D0537726

MARK BRANDI

the rip

Legend Press Ltd, 51 Gower Street, London, WC1E 6HJ
info@legend-paperbooks.co.uk | www.legendpress.co.uk

Contents © Mark Brandi 2019
First published by Hachette Australia (an imprint of Hachette Australia Pty
Limited), Level 17, 207 Kent Street, Sydney NSW 2000
www.hachette.com.au

Print ISBN 978-1-78955-1-112
Ebook ISBN 978-1-78955-1-129
Set in Times. Production managed by Jellyfish Solutions Ltd.
Cover design by Rose Cooper | www.rosecooper.com

All characters, other than those clearly in the public domain, and place
names, other than those well-established such as towns and cities, are
fictitious and any resemblance is purely coincidental.

All rights reserved. No part of this publication may be reproduced, stored
in or introduced into a retrieval system, or transmitted, in any form, or by
any means electronic, mechanical, photocopying, recording or otherwise,
without the prior permission of the publisher. Any person who commits any
unauthorised act in relation to this publication may be liable to criminal
prosecution and civil claims for damages.

After initially studying law, then completing a degree in criminal justice, **Mark Brandi** worked extensively in corrections and emergency services before turning his hand to writing. His shorter pieces appear in *The Guardian, The Age, The Big Issue*, and in journals both in Australia and overseas. His writing is sometimes heard on Australia's ABC Radio National.

Originally from Italy, growing up in a rural Australian town (in a pub) continues to influence his creative focus. He now lives in Melbourne. His debut novel, *Into the River*, was published by Legend Press in 2019.

Follow Mark at
www.markbrandi.com
or on Twitter
@mb_randi

For Georgia

Now, where were we?

You tell me.

We were talking about what was found in your room.

You were talking about it.

Some sort of chemical, right?

No idea.

You don't know what it is?

Nah.

Was in your room, you know.

So?

It's not a big room.

I know that.

Stinks something terrible.

My room?

The chemical.

Didn't really notice.

How'd it get there?

Dunno. Already there, I spose.

In the room?

Yep. When I moved in.

Which was when?

Couple of months back.

Never thought to ask what it was?

Why would I?

Well, forensics are looking at it now.

Right.

We'll get the answer, one way or another.

If you say so.

Back to the girl then.
What about her?
Care to tell us what happened?
Already told ya.
We've just checked those places, mate. No record.
Dunno then. Must be a mistake.
No mistake.
No kidding.
CCTV is coming. Should have it in the next hour.
And?
Well, you can see where this is heading, can't ya?
No idea.
Look, mate, accidents happen.
That's true.
We're not here to judge.
Fair enough.
So why don't you just tell us, yeah? What happened?

before

before

one

Anton wakes me. He's always first up in the morning. A real early riser.

'Getting up?'

'Piss off,' I say.

He lies down beside me, like he's trying to spoon me. But not in a sexual way or anything. He's not like that, Anton. Never tried anything on me, which is good.

'You were back late last night,' he says.

I can feel his breath on my neck.

'C'mon. Sun's shining, birds are singing.'

I pull the sleeping bag up over my head.

'C'mon,' he says, and pulls it back down.

'Rack off.'

He laughs and starts tickling me, which he knows I can't stand. It's like bloody torture, but I kind of love it too. Sometimes.

I start wriggling, and Sunny comes in and he's licking my face, and I realise it's all pretty much no use. I sit up slowly.

It's cold, and I keep the sleeping bag up to my chin with one hand. My bra strap is digging in something fierce, so I reach up under my t-shirt.

Anton smiles. He has pretty good teeth compared to most in the park – a bit yellow, but none missing or busted.

He waves around one of those squeegee things, like the

window washers use. 'Look at this, will ya?' he says, tilting it to the light. 'Our ticket to fame and fortune.'

He starts laughing, but it becomes a cough pretty quick.

'Where'd you get it?'

'Servo on Victoria Street. One with the 7-Eleven.' He pats Sunny, coughs again. 'C'mon, know a good spot. Easy money.'

'Nah.'

'C'mon. If we get there by peak hour, we'll smash it.'

I can see he's had a bit of a wash under the tap, because his hair is wet and slicked back a bit. He reckons he's the bees knees, looks-wise. He told me once how girls used to say he looked like Dave Navarro from the Red Hot Chili Peppers, but I reckon he probably made that up. I know the Red Hot Chili Peppers, but I don't know which one Dave Navarro is. I did like that 'Under the Bridge' song, though.

I need a piss something terrible, so I put Sunny on the rope. The toilets at the park are pretty crap and stink a bit. They have one of those stainless steel mirrors that's scratched to shit. I suppose it isn't glass so teenagers can't break it, but a steel mirror is pretty pointless. At least they clean the joint every couple of days, and the women's ones are pretty quiet mostly. But not so much on the weekends, because that's when the parents come with their kids and do the whole happy families thing with barbecues and frisbees and all that.

Anton reckons he needs a piss too. He doesn't like using the men's ones so much, because he reckons they're a beat. That's where guys meet sometimes to jerk each other off and give blowjobs and that kind of stuff. He isn't into that sort of thing, which is fair enough, though I wonder how he knows about it.

I get Anton to wait outside with Sunny. It isn't like Sunny will run away or anything, but I'm worried that someone might nick him.

I put toilet paper on the seat, which is something I've always done. And not just in public toilets either. It's just more hygienic, I reckon, and it feels better on your arse. Especially when it's cold. I don't know why more people don't do it.

After, I wash my hands carefully and the water is nice and cool on my skin. I put my mouth under the tap and have a long drink. It tastes a bit metallic and I need to get a toothbrush something terrible – it's been ages.

Anton calls out, 'Hurry up, will ya?'

'Yep, all right.'

I have a look at myself in the mirror, but I can't see much because, besides being scratched, it's a bit warped – almost like something from a carnival.

Probably just as well.

* * *

Anton says we should go to Victoria Street, because there are like eight lanes there, and we're sure to make some cash.

'What am I supposed to do?' I say.

'Keep me company. And keep an eye out for the cops. You can get the water too, if you want.'

He doesn't have a bucket or anything, so he fishes an empty water bottle out of a bin. It's one of those ones with the funny top, so you can squeeze it out.

'What about detergent?'

He looks at me all stunned, wide-eyed, like he hasn't even thought of it.

'Don't need it,' he says. 'Water's enough.'

That doesn't sound right, so I'm guessing he's never actually done window washing before. I mean, it isn't like something you need training for, but detergent seems pretty obvious.

'You know what you're doing?' I say.

'Yeah. Used to be a shearer, remember?'

'What's that got to do with it?'

He shrugs.

Anton had told me soon after I met him about how he used to be a shearer. That was why he was used to getting up early – a routine that kind of stuck. But he got in a bad fight once, which is why he went to jail. And when he got out, he had no one. All of that's true, he says.

He's not on the gear or nothing, just booze and pills mostly. Fentanyl or Endone. Hillbilly Heroin, some people call it. And he smokes.

Here's the thing with smokes – and this is completely bizarre – they've gotten really expensive. Worse than being on the gear, which is pretty mental if you think about it. I've never been into smoking much. Bit of dope, but that used to make me paranoid. Full on. Especially on the bong.

Anton points over to the tram shelter. 'You wait there. I'll let you know when I need more water.'

'Where am I gonna get it?'

He frowns and gives me this look, which is like – *that's your job*.

A lot of people just wave him off at first. So I tell him he has to give them 'the free one'. That's what Mick – who was this old hippy who stayed at the park (he's dead now) – that's what he used to do. He used to give them 'the free one', and then some of them would feel guilty and give him some coins. He used to do pretty well out of it, and always had plenty of good gear. Which was actually what killed him in the end.

Anton tries 'the free one', and he starts getting money probably two out of three times. I add it up and I reckon we have about thirty bucks so far, which isn't too bad.

'Would've done better with Eftpos,' he says. 'No one has cash anymore.'

'Maybe dealers might start taking Eftpos too.'

He laughs.

I find a tap in the garden of this old church, which is right on the corner of the intersection. I've taken Sunny over with me for a drink. It isn't that warm or nothing, but he's panting like he's thirsty, and he's probably getting a bit hungry too.

But before I can even open the tap, I hear Anton yelling out. I turn around and he's sprinting across the road like a mental case.

'Run!' he says. 'For fuck's sake, run!'

He bolts towards me, eyes like saucers.

Up the road, I see a divvy van flying down the tram tracks with lights flashing, but no sirens. Maybe one of the drivers called the cops, which is pretty shitful. Or maybe the cops were headed somewhere else. I mean, window washing isn't the crime of the century or nothing, but Anton has a bad record so can't risk getting caught for anything.

Me and Anton and Sunny run behind the church, then down a lane, and we get behind some houses before we stop to catch our breath. After a bit, Anton starts laughing.

'It's not funny,' I say.

'Don't worry. They won't come looking for us.'

Still, we wait a while, until we're sure they'll be gone.

Turns out Anton dropped the squeegee somewhere when we were running. We look, but can't find it. I count up the money again and it's $35.40 exactly, which is pretty good. He gives me half for getting the water, which means I just need another twenty.

'How you gonna get it?' he says.

'How do you reckon?'

He hesitates, scratches his chin. 'Want some more then?'

'Why?'

'So you don't have to... you know.'

That's the thing – Anton doesn't like me turning tricks so much. He doesn't even like talking about it. It isn't like he's my boyfriend or anything, or that he's jealous, but it's still pretty obvious he doesn't like it. It's probably because he's seen some of the trouble it can cause me.

'I'll manage,' I say.

* * *

We go down Victoria Street to the shopping centre, because I remember I need to get a toothbrush.

'You wait outside,' I say.

'Why?'

I give Sunny a pat. 'Someone has to stay with him.'

I don't mention it, but there's also this security bloke who works in the shopping centre and he's a bit of a dick. If it's just me on my own, I won't be as likely to get followed. But with two of us, it looks completely suss.

I head to Aldi because it never seems like they have much staff working. It's really bright in there, and I notice how they don't have any music playing – which is a bit weird – but I can't remember if it's always like that. Coles and Woolworths and those places have music on all the time, and it's nearly always shit.

I go to the back of the Aldi because that's where the toiletries and stuff are. I get a toothbrush – a red one with soft bristles for my gums – and shove it down the back of my undies. Suddenly, I need a piss something terrible, which always seems to happen when I'm nicking something.

There's a few strange things about Aldi, like the chainsaws and gym equipment and random stuff they sell sometimes. Another thing is you can't get out except by going past one of the checkouts, so I always pick one which is pretty busy.

There's one with a Muslim who has a trolley full of stuff – cans and bottles and all sorts – like she must have twenty kids or something. A skinny bloke is working the checkout and looks pretty new, a bit slow and unsure, so I walk around the Muslim as quick as I can, and the skinny checkout bloke says, 'Excuse me', and I can tell he's saying it to me, but I keep walking like I don't hear him. Which is – so you know – exactly how you do it.

But then, someone grabs me hard, very hard. Hurting my arm. *Shit.*

'What you got?'

The security bloke. He smells like aftershave or deodorant or too much hair gel.

'Fuck off.'

This probably isn't the smartest thing to say, but he's really hurting my arm.

He grips me harder, smiles, and pulls me in close.

'Listen, you junkie fuck, if I see you back here again, I'll smash your teeth in. Understand?'

He says it rough and hot and breathy in my ear, and slides his hand up between my legs and squeezes me there. He gets me so hard it hurts.

I shake loose and run up the escalator, past some teenagers who are heading up to Daiso to buy some Jap shit. Daiso is this place that sells everything for $2.80. Anton reckons it's almost like getting it for free, but not quite.

The toilets up near Daiso are new and nearly always clean. It's all dark grey tile and sparkling chrome. They have one of those fragrance spray things on the wall, and a fancy Dyson hand dryer, and I suddenly feel like I need a long hot shower more than almost anything in the world.

I stop in front of the mirror, which is a proper one this time. I take off my beanie and my hair is a bit greasy, but not too bad. My skin looks dry, but no pimples or sores or nothing. I don't need to piss anymore, so I get the toothbrush out of my undies, rinse it under the tap, and give my teeth a good go until my gums start bleeding.

Even though it hurts, my mouth feels much better after. I look at myself, then into my eyes for a bit. Probably too long. And it makes me wonder if my eyes are like what hers were like.

And I decide they are, that mine are exactly the same colour. Even if there's no way I could ever remember.

two

Anton is over the other side of the road with Sunny, talking to one of the dealers. I know he's a dealer, because I used to buy off him.

His name is Paul, but I've never thought that's actually his real name. He's Vietnamese and has thick oily hair and long fingernails. Makes me want to be somewhere clean.

'Hey Paul,' I say.

He smiles, but not with his eyes.

'Long time, no see,' he says.

'Busy.'

Anton kneels down and scratches Sunny behind both ears at once, which he loves. He rolls onto his back like it's all too much.

Paul watches them both, then eyes me.

'If you ever want to offload him,' he says, 'let me know.'

'Who?'

'The dog.'

'Sunny?'

He nods. 'Give you cash. Or some gear.'

'Nah.'

He shrugs. 'Offer's there.'

Anton sees my look.

'Paul was just talking about a murder,' he says. 'Up in the flats.'

'Yeah?' I say.

Paul nods.

'Go on, tell her.'

Paul looks out over the road, to somewhere in the middle distance. He's the sort who never holds your gaze, which I suppose goes with the territory.

'Some old guy,' he says. 'Took out his eyes. Pair of scissors.'

'Fuck,' I say. 'Who did it?'

'Sixteen-year-old kid. Skinny little thing. Rumour is the old bloke was touching her up.' Paul laughs from somewhere down in his throat. 'Not so much now.'

'Cops got her?'

Paul looks up the street. A nervous tradie in a Bunnings t-shirt pretending to look for the best bok choy – he nods at Paul. Paul reaches into his pocket.

'Gotta go,' he says.

I take Sunny by the rope and me and Anton head the other way, towards the city. To be honest, I'm pretty pleased to get away from Paul, but I don't say so.

Up the street, one of the greengrocers gives me and Sunny a filthy look and says something really fast in Vietnamese. So Anton nicks a bunch of bananas from the stand out front, which is probably a bit cheeky. But I'm happy he does it.

People give Sunny dirty looks all the time, mainly because he's a bull terrier. It's pretty crap really. I mean, it's the owners that are the problem, not the dogs – that's what Anton says.

Bull terriers have got a beautiful nature. Sunny is white, except for a tan patch over one eye. I called him Sunny because it was sunny the day I got him. I know that it isn't very clever or anything, but it suits him perfect.

We stop at Hoddle Street because Anton is coughing his guts out. I eat one of the bananas and it's a bit starchy, but okay. Anton bends over like he's about to spew. I look up the road for a tram, but none are coming. And we've got Sunny anyway, so only Anton would be able to get on. No dogs allowed on trams, unless you've got one of those tiny ones that people sometimes have in their handbags, but they seem pretty pointless.

I wait till he stops coughing.

'What do you wanna do?'

He takes a few deep breaths in and out, spits, then reaches into his pocket.

'Here,' he says.

It's a baggie.

'How did you—?'

'Said I'll fix him up for the rest later. Knows I'm good for it.' I take it from his hand. Maybe a bit too quick.

'What about you?' I say.

He shrugs. 'Got some Endone. Half a pack.'

That's the thing with Anton – only ever the prescription stuff. Gets some of it doctor shopping, but from dealers now too. He reckons it's better for him, like he can control it better. He started using painkillers when he was shearing, for his back – that's what he tells me. He got on the gear for a bit too, when he was inside, but managed to kick it.

I hold the bag up to the light and study the pale, brown powder. As if I know what to look for, as if I can tell if something is not quite right.

'Jeez, don't be so suspicious,' he says.

'But last time it—'

'I made him promise.'

See, that's why I don't buy off Paul anymore. Not because of his oily hair, his shifty eyes, or even those long, yellow fingernails that have started to curl. The last time I bought off him, I got really sick. Like, I could hardly move. Whatever it was, it wasn't smack. He sells a bit of ice too, mostly to the tradies, but it definitely wasn't that either.

Anton lights a smoke. 'Got a different supplier now,' he says. 'Some bikies. Much purer, so he reckons.'

* * *

Normally, I'd wait till I got back to the park. I usually prefer to do it at home. It's just easier and means you don't have to worry about things. The logistics, I mean, like getting home after.

But the thing is, when you've got some gear in your pocket, you just can't stop thinking about it. Even though you're happy you've got some, it makes you more anxious, and makes you want it more, because it's right there at your fingertips.

Anton holds onto Sunny out in the street. It's hard to find a quiet spot, a laneway where there's no traffic, or no one walking past. It isn't like I'm ashamed or nothing, but I'd just prefer not to have anyone gawking at me.

But Jesus.

The thing about when you get a good hit is how it makes everything much clearer than you could ever imagine. It's impossible to describe properly, but it's like something beautiful and warm is filling you up, smoothing off all the rough edges. The crawling skin, the knot in your belly, the worry – all of it gone.

I don't want to make it sound romantic. Except *it is* romantic. And it's just about the most wonderful thing there is. I love it. And it's something I'll always love, probably as long as I live. I suppose it's a bit like smokers – maybe that's a good way for people to think about it. Smokers might quit smoking because of all the other shit that goes with it, but the actual smoking part is something they enjoy – something they might always love. But they just make a rational decision, I suppose, that the downside isn't worth it.

But for me, the downside *is* worth it. Because downside is pretty much all I've ever known. Getting high is my only glimpse of the upside, if that makes sense.

'Isn't that true?' I say.

Anton shoots me this look. 'What?'

'What I've been saying?'

'You haven't been saying anything.'

'About smoking.'

He grins. 'You're high.'

'Jeez, who do you think you are? Dave Navarro?'

So I try to explain it all to Anton, but he just looks at me and laughs. He tells me again that I'm high, and this time I agree.

And he thinks that's just about the funniest thing ever.

'Aldi don't have any music,' I say.

'Really?'

'So you can concentrate on your shopping.'

'Didn't know that.'

'And you have to pack your own bags.'

He's walking slow and so is Sunny, and the sky is yellow and soft and warm.

'They have music at Coles,' I say.

'The "Down Down" song?'

'Nah, Coles radio. "Slice of Heaven" is their favourite.'

'Whose favourite?'

'The DJ.'

'There is no DJ.'

'The Coles DJ. There's a countdown.'

'It's just a recording.'

'Don't think so.'

'It is. Anyway, it's "Come on Eileen".'

'What?'

'Their favourite.'

He tries to sing the lyrics, and it's awful and hilarious.

And we walk for ages in the warm sun, with the sweet breeze tickling my skin, and Sunny right beside me.

We walk and walk, like it doesn't matter where we're going. We walk like we might just keep going on forever.

three

It must be close to autumn, because some of the trees in the park are losing their leaves. And it's starting to get cooler.

Coming down always makes me feel colder than I should be. The same as when you're sick or really tired, I suppose. I sit next to Sunny and wrap myself and him in the sleeping bag. Anton sits next to me.

A group of boys, carrying a slab of beer, walk past slowly – pretending not to look. They murmur among themselves, but don't say anything out loud. Anton eyes them closely.

Couple of weeks back, a few teenagers hassled one of the old blokes – Johnny, I think his name is. Doesn't talk much. And they started kicking his stuff around like it was a big joke and he got pretty upset. It was Anton who scared them off.

The boys open their slab and pass around a couple of beers. They keep walking.

'Should try to get out of here,' Anton says.

'What?'

'The park. Should try to get a flat.'

He always gets talking like this when the weather starts to turn. And I always tell him the same thing.

'Housing people won't give me one. Not after last time.'

'But this would be different. You wouldn't be doing that anymore.'

That's part of it, I think. Anton hates me working, which is what got me kicked out in the first place. The neighbours were complaining about blokes coming round, which is probably fair enough. But I was just trying to get by, and they couldn't mind their own business.

'You could do your zoo thing,' Anton says.

The 'zoo thing' was something I'd said just once, but he's really hung onto it. Never forgotten about it.

When I was at school, there was this animal petting zoo that came and visited, and we got to pat horses and dogs and rabbits, and even a dingo.

Anton reckons we could do something like that one day, and travel around the country visiting schools.

'Sunny could be the star attraction,' he says.

I don't think he's really thought it through properly.

'And we could get a proper flat. With a little backyard and everything.'

'We could,' I say, mostly to make him feel better. But I'm not really thinking about that.

Thing is, when you're straight, you get the craving. The craving is the first bit, where you just need to feel it again, that warmth flowing like waves inside you. Anton says it's a kind of euphoria, a rush, even though he's only on prescription stuff and doesn't get it as strong.

But if you don't get on it fast enough, the craving just gets more intense. Every other thought gets pushed out of your head, and all you can think about is where you're gonna get some money and how you're gonna score. Like almost nothing else matters, and nothing can get in your way.

But once you do get back on, the craving is worth it. It's not like relief, it's so much more than that – it's all about now, what you're seeing and feeling. Truly, unless you've had it, you could never know how much pleasure your body can feel.

That's the best bit about getting high, and probably what a lot of people don't understand. It can make you forget about the past, that's true. But all that pleasure stops you worrying about what's coming.

The very first time was different. The first time was more like this warm, tingling rush through my whole body – it was beautiful and unexpected.

It's still beautiful, but different. But I think it's different for everyone, and even different each time. And that's what Anton reckons too.

'Depends on your biochemistry,' he says, but I'm not really sure exactly what that means. To be honest, I don't think I could ever make you understand what it's like for me, unless you could be me for a minute, just so you could feel it.

For a while, it's like you're always chasing that feeling – trying to get it back again. But then, before you even realise it, it becomes something else. You still want that pleasure inside you, the rush, but also a kind of absence from everything. A disconnection. Like you can just float above it.

When you're coming down though, it's different. More like a kind of temporary depression, I suppose. Most people feel sick, but for me it's more about the sadness. Like a dull, heavy weight in my guts. So it's good to have Anton around, but somehow kind of bittersweet too. I'm not sure why, not exactly.

Anton always does most of the talking. I like when he talks about how jail was, which is probably the thing he talks about the least. Usually only if I ask. But I have to be careful about how I do it, so it's not too obvious.

He lights a smoke.

'You were supposed to be quitting.'

He shrugs.

'It's expensive.'

'Yep.'

'How long's it been?'

'What?'

'That you've been smoking.'

He takes a long drag. 'Since I went inside.'

I pause. Sunny lets out a long sigh like he's about to go to sleep, like he's heard all of this too many times.

'Ever think about that bloke?'

'Which bloke?' he says.

'You know.'

'Who?' He stubs out his smoke on the ground.

'The one you killed.'

He frowns. 'Where did that come from?'

I give Sunny a pat. 'I mean, do you feel bad about it? Like, for his family and that?'

He coughs. 'Course I feel bad. Yeah. But I didn't mean it, you know?'

And that was the thing. Anton reckons he didn't mean to kill him. It was a bloke he worked with, another shearer.

'Alicia – we both liked her.'

I always think it's a bit funny that it was about a girl. Not that Anton is gay or nothing. At least, not that I know of. He isn't gay or straight, as far as I can tell. Like I said, he's never tried anything on me. Never even looks at me like that, or talks about it. It's like he just isn't into sex at all.

'I just hit him once, his head hit the floor. And that was it.'

They got him for manslaughter. But because he pleaded guilty, and he was young, the judge gave him a pretty light sentence. Out after five.

'Worst years of my life.'

I know all this story, of course, but I still like listening again. I know it all pretty much back to front, which is why I notice how it sometimes changes a bit. Not in big ways, but in little ways that I don't think he even realises.

Like, this time, he calls the girl 'Alicia'. You'd think he'd get that right. Last time, I'm sure it was Amanda. Pretty sure, anyway.

I never say anything about it, though. I like Anton. And honestly, I never thought he could be violent like that. Not in his nature.

But, I suppose you never really know everything about people.

'Hungry?' he says.

'Nah.'

'Still, we probably should.'

Good thing about sleeping at Princes Park, compared to some of the other spots, is there aren't many people who sleep here. So you get a fair bit of privacy. But the downside is that none of the Salvos or anyone ever come with the soup van. Most of that happens in the city, but the city has some pretty major downsides too.

Anton stands up. 'Bakers Delight?'

'Again?'

'Got a better idea?'

Sometimes Anton cooks for us. There's a big community garden at the Abbotsford Convent, and a couple of the people there are really nice and give him some of their vegies. I'm not big on vegies so much, but I like when he gets potatoes. He does this thing where he slices them super thin, then cooks them on the barbecue in the park, in hot oil and salt. They're really delicious. He's a pretty good cook, Anton. Reckons he learned how when he was shearing. I don't really understand the link, but haven't bothered to ask.

Anyway, there's no chance of fried potatoes right now.

* * *

There's a shopping centre not far from the park, and it has one of those horrible bakeries there. I hate that stuff – it all tastes like onion and processed cheese, and it makes me think about fat people who sit around in shopping centres all day, eating Bakers Delight. But the one good thing is they never keep stuff from the previous day.

I keep an eye out for security, because they don't like people going through the bins even though they're throwing it all out, which is kind of ridiculous. Anton climbs up inside the skip and disappears. Pretty quickly, he's back up on the edge with a black garbage bag. Reaches inside.

'Pizza roll? Or... a pizza roll?'

'Two please.'

I give one to Sunny, who nearly takes the whole thing in one go. I eat my one, but can hardly taste it. Being on the gear does that to you. Like, it dulls some of the senses. Especially taste and smell, which is probably just as well, actually.

Anton perches on the edge of the skip, looking like a skinny rat. He chews down another roll, dangles his legs like a kid. I suddenly wonder what he would have been like when he was young. What he looked like, and if he was happy.

He eyes me, frowns. 'You all right?'

I kneel down and give Sunny a hug. He stiffens like he doesn't really like it, but I pretend not to notice. I nuzzle into his neck and feel his warmth against my skin.

'Hey, you two!'

I turn around and a man is walking quickly across the car park towards us – a skinny Indian guy who looks about my age, but it's hard sometimes to tell with those people.

Anton drops the garbage bag into the skip, slips off the edge and back onto the ground.

I should've been keeping an eye out.

The guy's wearing a white shirt and black pants, and talking into a walkie-talkie type thing, like he's a secret agent or something.

'You cannot be here,' he says.

'Okay, okay,' Anton says. He brushes his hands together, cleaning off the crumbs. 'We're going, mate. No need for trouble.'

The Indian puts the walkie-talkie back in his pocket.

'Private property,' he says. 'I call the police if I see you again.'

'We get the message,' Anton says.

I take Sunny by his rope, shoot the Indian a look.

'What difference does it make?' I say.

I feel my face going hot. Anton takes my arm, eyes me, shakes his head.

'Easy,' he says.

I pull from his grip. 'Seriously,' I say, 'what difference does it make to you? It's all in the fucking rubbish anyway. And we're not hurting anyone, are we?'

The Indian's eyes go wide and he gets his walkie-talkie out again.

'C'mon,' Anton says. 'Let's go.'

He says it close to my ear, quiet, so I can feel his breath. Like he means it.

'Not worth it,' he says. 'And besides, I've got a much better idea.'

four

Anton isn't religious or anything. Not at all. I remember he told me once how he went to a Catholic school in the country, but it was completely shit. That's pretty much all he ever said about it.

But he knows a fair bit about the Abbotsford Convent. He knows about it because he once stayed in a hostel right near it. He reckons that hostel was good, but too expensive, so he went to the one in the city. And that was where I first met him.

It wasn't a proper hostel or nothing – just an old pub with really cheap rooms. They were really cheap for a reason though, run-down as hell. And none of the locks worked properly.

There was a bloke there named Gus. He was Greek or Italian or something, and was just a major stoner who'd been living there forever. Anyway, I wasn't planning on staying very long, because he was cracking onto me constantly. Hassling me for sex.

One night, he just went for it. He came into my room, got on top of me, and started pulling off my knickers. I screamed out, but he wouldn't stop.

Shhh... Shhh... I won't take long.

His breath was meaty, like lamb. He stuck his fingers in rough and started licking my ear. His dick was limp and he was trying to get me to wank it, and that's when Anton burst through the door.

I didn't know then that his name was Anton – I'd seen him around, but hadn't met him. So it was a pretty good turn he did for me, I reckon.

There were a lot of people who would've known what was happening, people who heard me scream, people who knew me.

There were people who spoke to me every day, who acted like they were my friend. But they didn't do a thing.

Only Anton.

* * *

The convent used to be where they sent girls who got pregnant, or were a bit off the rails. Anton reckons even the courts used to send them there, and the nuns had this whole thing set up where they got the girls as free labour. They had a big laundry and the girls did all the sheets and stuff for the rich people in Melbourne, and the nuns made heaps of money out of it.

Life must've been pretty shit for the girls. Anton reckons I would have ended up there for sure, if I'd been around in the olden days.

I don't know if it's completely true about the nuns and the laundry, but I like going to the convent, so I try not to think about it too much.

It's this big old building and it has a bakery and nice gardens and heaps of room for Sunny to run. There's even the Yarra down the back, but Anton says it's polluted. The nuns aren't around anymore, and there isn't anything religious going on, I don't think.

There's this place called 'Lentil as Anything' where you can get food and you only pay what you can afford to. That's a pretty sweet deal. It isn't like the Salvos or anything, but more like some kind of hippy thing, because there are usually a lot of that sort at the convent. And the occasional weirdo from the hostel.

The food is all vego and it has a bit too much onion and garlic for my liking, but you're not fussy when you're paying bugger all. Speaking of, this time Anton offers to pay, which is pretty good.

The whole thing is done through a charity box, so you can sneak out easy enough, which I think most people do.

'Maybe don't bother,' I say. 'They won't know either way.'

But Anton isn't like that. Even the times when we'd spent nearly all our dole, he still pays. Like I said, he isn't into God or anything, but sometimes he acts like a religious person, like someone who thinks you should always do the right thing. He has these rules – it's almost like he believes that if you do the right thing, your life works out better. Something like that.

Maybe that's true. But maybe it isn't, and then you'd waste your time trying to be nice, even though the world is pretty rotten.

I'm probably not much of a philosopher, and that's probably not a very positive way to think about things, but it's how I feel sometimes.

I should explain something quick, just while I think of it. I should say about Anton's dad, because I think it might explain why he is the way he is. Partly, anyway.

His dad's name was Sid, and in the town where Anton grew up, his dad was in some sort of mental hospital. Sid was an alcoholic and his brain was ruined, so people in town called him Silly Sid.

When he was a kid, Anton used to visit him at the mental hospital, which would have been pretty awful. Anyway, they eventually shut down the place and Silly Sid got moved into a house with an old man who looked after him. But the old man wasn't a nurse or anything – he only did it so he could get extra money from the government.

So Silly Sid was living with the old man, but the old man

was also an alcoholic, so whoever decided to put Sid there probably wasn't thinking very hard about how it might end up.

Anton told me he visited his dad a few times before he died, and it wasn't very good. Like, he'd shat himself and hadn't been cleaned for days, and the old man and him were both just drinking themselves to death. And that's what happened to Silly Sid in the end.

Anyway, maybe this explains why Anton likes to have rules about things. Maybe because his dad didn't have any.

* * *

There are a couple of hostel people at the end of our table. You can pick them out right away, mainly because they're much older than everyone else, but also the clothes.

They're wearing sports gear even though they clearly aren't sporty-looking types. It's definitely donated stuff that's about twenty years too young for them.

Even more than the clothes, you can tell from the eyes. Not like they're on it or anything, but how they avoid eye contact. Like that's something they learnt inside, to avoid trouble, and they can't stop doing it once they're out. Not that you'd want to make eye contact with them anyway, I don't think.

They both have that old-fashioned convict look that some crooks have, with sunken eyes and thin, sour-looking mouths. One has his head shaved right to the skin, with a few nicks like it was just done fresh.

'Know them?' I say.

Anton shakes his head.

'Revolving door at that joint.'

The food is okay. We get dessert too, which is a chocolate fudge that's ridiculously sweet, but I eat it anyway. Anton reckons all the food is made by refugees or something, like I should be more understanding, but I don't really care much about that.

The two hostel men finish their food without saying a

word. The bald one nods to the other, and they both go to leave. I wonder if they were in the same prison together, and if maybe they used to do exactly the same thing at meal times. I watch to see if they pay or not, because I'm sure they won't. But then the bald one puts a few coins in the donation box. He makes a bit of a show of it, almost like he knew I was watching.

People can surprise you sometimes, but not usually. Most of the time, people act exactly as you'd expect.

So maybe I was wrong. Maybe they weren't hostel people after all.

* * *

There are a couple of hippies outside under a tree, and they're patting Sunny like he's the greatest dog they've ever seen.

Hippies probably like Sunny the most of all people. Hippies and crooks, I think. Young mums with little kids probably like him the least, especially at the park and especially if their kids are toddlers. The ones with babies in prams are okay, but the ones with toddlers usually freak when they see him, like they think Sunny is gonna run up and bite the kid's head off.

It pisses me off, the way they look at him. Even more than the way they look at me.

The mums with babies in prams usually just ignore us, or sometimes smile at me in the way people smile at someone who's a bit retarded. That pisses me off too. Actually, young mums kind of piss me off in general, like they think rooting and getting pregnant is some kind of miracle that hasn't already happened about a hundred million times.

But maybe I'm a bit negative about it all. 'A pessimist' – that's what Anton says. I think I'm just being realistic.

One of the hippies is this guy with thick dreadlocks, which you don't see much anymore. He crouches down with Sunny and says, 'You're a good boy,' and the girl says to me, 'Your dog is amazing,' and they've both got German accents or something, and I'm pretty certain they're both majorly stoned.

She has long dark hair, and he is all brown-skinned and beautiful, and they both have the best teeth I have ever seen in my life.

'Thanks,' I say.

'What's his name?'

'Sunny.'

'Oh, Sunny!' She rubs his chest. 'So, so beautiful.' She smiles at me. 'Are you coming to the movie too?'

I untie Sunny's rope. 'What movie?'

She reaches into her bag and pulls out a crumpled flyer. 'Outdoor cinema,' she says. She hands it to me, then points somewhere out behind the convent. 'On later. You should come!'

I suddenly remember seeing the posters around. I turn to Anton. 'What do you think?'

He shrugs. 'Depends what's on.'

The guy with dreadies slaps Anton on the shoulder, which I can tell pisses him off. A flash of anger in his eyes, but he tries to hide it.

'Spanish movie,' the German says. 'I've seen it, man. Really brilliant!'

'Maybe.' Anton eyes me. 'But we should head down to the community garden first.'

'That's cool,' the girl says. 'Do what you gotta do, yeah? Starts at dusk.'

* * *

We can't get any vegies. There are some gardeners there, but they're people we haven't seen before, so we don't feel like we can ask.

It's mostly old people who have plots, and they sometimes die or end up in the nursing home, but you only ever find out about that when someone else takes over their plot.

It's a bit disappointing. I can see the raspberries have started to ripen, and they're one of my favourite things.

'You wanna go see it?' Anton says.

'What?'

'You know. The movie.'

I shrug. 'Might be all right.'

Anton nods. 'Yeah, maybe.'

'Would we have to pay?'

'Doubt it.'

'Maybe we should then.'

He frowns. 'Okay, but let's sit on our own though.'

'What? You don't like the hippies?'

He smiles, embarrassed. 'They're all right. But I just don't feel like... you know.'

I do know. He doesn't need to say it.

He means the thing with people, when they find out where we live. They always ask, because it's one of those things people do. It's not like we're ashamed of it, but most people give you these eyes which make you feel pretty terrible. Anton says it's pity, and he reckons pity is about the worst insult you can get. He's probably right about that. It's definitely worse than the looks from the young mums.

You might think that feeling sorry for people is helpful, but it's not. It's actually one of the worst things there is.

* * *

As it turns out, we do have to pay to watch the movie. So we wait for a while, until it's completely dark, before we sneak in. It's down behind the convent, near the river. There's no fences or anything, so it's pretty easy. And there's a lot of people just watching the screen, so no one seems to notice, except this one lady on a picnic blanket who gives Sunny a bit of a look, then says something to her boyfriend or husband or whatever.

Maybe you're not supposed to have dogs there, or maybe she just doesn't like the look of us, but I pretend not to notice.

And I don't say anything to Anton about it, because I don't want to ruin things.

We find a spot up near the back, behind some people with foldout chairs and bottles of wine, and we sit on the grass with Sunny. Can't see the hippies anywhere, which is probably just as well.

The movie is called *Pan's Labyrinth*, and we both really like it. It's in Spanish, but with subtitles, so it's easy enough to follow. And it's really lovely to sit outside in the open and watch it like that. Especially because Sunny gets to sit with us too, which is probably the best bit, even if he starts snoring about halfway through.

Anton says it reminds him of going to the drive-in when he was a kid, 'But better'. He reckons we'll definitely do it again sometime.

We both agree that it's an excellent movie, but the only thing we disagree about is what happens at the end. But I won't tell you about that now, just in case you haven't seen it.

It's really beautiful, so I wouldn't want to ruin it.

five

Anton reckons we should go to Centrelink. It's pretty much the first thing he says to me when I wake up.

'If we get there early, we'll miss the queues and all that.'

Sunny is asleep beside me. I roll over and nuzzle in close.

'C'mon,' he says.

'What for?'

'The flat. See if we can get on the list.'

I really can't be bothered, but he seems a bit fired up about it – not in an aggressive way, just a bit hyper. Like it's suddenly really important.

Thing is, there's hardly any Centrelinks around anymore. There used to be a good one on Johnston Street, but it's some kind of nightclub now. It was good because there was this Chilean bloke, and he was always really nice to me. Treated me normal.

But then they all got merged into these kind of mega-stores with Medicare and childcare and everything in one place. Anton says they're trying to save money. He also says that the nearest one is in Coburg, which takes about an hour to walk to.

'We'll just get the tram,' he says.

'Can't. With Sunny, I mean.'

'Just tie him up somewhere.'

This pisses me off a bit. Sunny's more than a dog to me,

and Anton knows it. Sunny's the main reason I won't go into shelters or anything, apart from all the freaks that are there.

'Nah,' I say. 'Just go on your own then.'

He's a bit pissed off too, I can tell. Anton always tries hard not to show he's upset, but I can tell when he is. Mostly because he won't look me in the eyes.

'C'mon then,' he says, 'we'll walk.'

It's gonna be a long way. And I'm pretty desperate to have a shower, which we usually do at the Salvos in Bourke Street, or at St Mary's in Fitzroy. St Mary's used to be run by nuns, but now it's mostly volunteers and churchy types. Anton prefers the Salvos, because he reckons the showers are cleaner.

'We'll go after,' he says. 'Depending on what happens with the flat.'

I really don't think anything is gonna happen with Centrelink, or the flat, but I go along with it. Anton gets these things in his head sometimes, and it isn't like they're bad ideas, but they hardly ever go anywhere. Actually, now that I think about it, they never go anywhere.

'Are you sure it's worth it? I mean—'

'Yeah, and besides,' he loops the rope around Sunny's neck, 'the walk will do him good. Us too.'

I suppose it's better to have ideas about doing something than just sitting around and waiting for stuff to happen. That never really works.

* * *

There's a lot of cafés on Sydney Road nowadays, especially at the city end. Fancy joints with people wearing those round-frame glasses, like they think they're really cool or something.

Sydney Road used to be good, because it was a real mix of people, so no one would look at you funny or anything. But now, there's more of those people who give you the looks, like they're worried you're gonna ask them for money. Sometimes they pick up their phones off the table, or their bags off the ground. They're not very subtle about it.

Sunny stops for a drink at a café with marble tables and lipstick girls in black aprons and colourful tattoos. They've got a big stainless-steel bowl of water there, which is pretty nice. At one table, there's this little girl. She has dark hair, full cheeks, and soft pink lips.

I smile at her, but she looks at me funny. And the woman, who must be her mum, she smiles too, but in that kind way – it's how I said before, the smile for people who are a bit retarded, or in a wheelchair.

It still seems like miles to Centrelink and I'm starting to shiver, but not from the cold. On top of it, I stink. Not terrible, but not good either – just a bit in that salty way. I start to wonder if Anton even knows where the place is, but I don't say anything.

Further north, we go past the Muslim cafés with the hookah pipes and the men who look at me like I'm something under their shoe. I'm sure some of them are probably nice and that, but I just don't like how they look at me. It's even worse than the kind smiles, or the ones who worry about you asking for money. Not as bad as the pity, though.

'Hate those places,' I say.

'Why?'

'The Muslims. The men, I mean.'

He laughs. 'You're racist.'

Anton reckons I shouldn't be like that. He's from the country, and there were hardly any ethnics when he was growing up. He was good friends with one at school, though. A Chinese kid. And he got picked on for it.

'Real One Nation territory,' he says. 'Pauline Hanson and all that.'

I'm not into politics, so I just pretend to know what he's talking about.

* * *

It's almost lunchtime by the time we get there. The place is frigging packed, like there's a line out the door. The shivers have gone, but now the skin on my arms is itching something fierce.

'Stop scratching,' Anton says.

'It's eczema, I reckon.' My left arm starts to bleed.

'Go to the doctor then.'

Anton joins the end of the queue.

'I'll stay out here.'

'Nah,' he says. 'You've gotta come too.'

I don't want to leave Sunny outside on his own. But Anton says we both have to go.

'They'll be more sympathetic.'

That's what he reckons.

I suppose the sooner we get it over with, the sooner we can go into town and I can have a shower. And we might be able to score too.

Actually, the more I think about it, it would be better to score first, then have a shower. Because the more I think about it, the more my skin is itching, and the more I'd really like a hit something terrible.

* * *

I get Anton to sit near a window so I can keep an eye on Sunny.

He's just lying there on the concrete with the sun on him, and he looks pretty happy. He's getting a few pats from people coming in, which is what worries me about leaving him out there.

Like I was saying, he's the sort of dog that some people don't like, but certain people do like. And he's friendly and easy-going enough that he'd probably go off with anyone. Pretty trusting, I suppose.

This really skinny girl with major piercings pats him for ages. She's with some slimy-looking bloke, and he looks like he's pretty keen on Sunny too. So when the skinny girl comes in, I get up from my chair before I even realise what I'm doing. Anton tries to grab my arm, but I'm too quick.

'Stop patting my dog,' I say.

She gives me these big eyes – all innocent.

'What?'

'I know what you're up to,' I say.

'Dunno what you're talking about.'

'Go near him again, you're gonna cop it.'

Everyone goes quiet.

She goes to walk off, but I grab her shoulder.

'What the fu—?'

Thing is, I didn't realise they have security at Centrelink nowadays, just like at the shopping centres. They never used to have that at Johnston Street.

The security man doesn't ask me to leave. Instead, he grabs me by the arm, twists it behind my back, and pushes me out the door.

'Let me go, you cunt!'

Anton follows us outside. He says something, but I don't catch what it is.

He isn't very happy with how I've behaved, I don't think. Because he won't barely look at me. And then he doesn't say anything for ages.

* * *

At the Salvos, Anton has his shower first, so I wait outside on the steps with Sunny. I'm still desperate for a wash, but letting him go first was kind of like my way of saying sorry.

'Shouldn't have done it,' he said.

'I know.'

'We went all that way.'

'I didn't mean to.'

And that was true. I didn't mean to lose it like that. But it's because I'm feeling so edgy.

I watch all the suits go by. A lot of them look pretty miserable, I reckon. They just stare at their phones with their nice coats and heels and lipstick.

I sometimes wonder what it would be like to be one of them, but not very often. I wonder what it would be like to be going back to a desk somewhere, or to meetings, or whatever it is they do. It's like they're in another world in some ways. Like, we're all in this same city, walking the same streets, but somehow on completely different planets. I'm sure some of them are nice, maybe most of them, but it's hard to know for sure.

I suppose they've all got their own worries too, things going on in their lives, but they're different worries than mine. Not easier or anything, just different.

Anton says it's important not to judge people by how they look, and I reckon he's right about that. He says you can never know exactly what's going on inside other people, in their hearts, because we barely know what's going on in ourselves.

Or something like that.

Anton is taking ages. I pat Sunny and try my best not to think about scoring, which somehow makes it worse because I think about it even more – about how we're gonna get it, and it's gonna be good, and how Anton better hurry the fuck up.

When you're a bit strung out like that, everything else disappears. It's all you can think about, and your whole body is just craving it – from your skin down into your flesh and even the blood in your veins, deep inside your organs and through your bones and everything – every piece of you.

'Hey.'

I look up and there's this tall skinny bloke with a blond crew cut and dark woollen overcoat that's too heavy for the weather. He's standing on the steps and smoking a cigarette. He's got a nose ring. And I can tell right away that he thinks he's pretty hot shit.

'Hi,' I say.

'Your dog?'

'Yep.'

He nods, squints his eyes like blokes do. 'Nice.'

I really don't want to have a conversation with overcoat man, and I decide that if Anton doesn't come out soon, I'm just gonna go right in there. With Sunny and everything.

That's the thing with Anton, he's a bit vain. So I can just imagine him staring at himself in the mirror, shaving his goatee just right, so maybe people might think he's that Dave Navarro guy.

I should just go try to score myself, but I'd have to turn a trick first, which is tough during the day. And I'll have no one to hold Sunny for me.

The skinny bloke takes a hard drag from his cigarette, gets the pack out from the inside pocket of his coat.

'Want one?'

'Nah.'

'Don't smoke?'

'Bad for you.'

He breathes out a thick blue plume.

'So they say.'

Footsteps behind me.

'Hey.'

Finally. Anton. He stops on the steps and looks at overcoat man with wide eyes. Almost like he knows him.

Overcoat man says, 'Jesus Christ.'

Anton smiles and shakes his hand, almost like he's an old friend. But I see this flash across his eyes – it's only for a split second, but I notice. And I think he isn't very happy to see the man in the overcoat, but he's trying not to show it.

I don't think overcoat man realises. It's subtle. And you'd only know it if you knew Anton really well.

six

So it's like Anton suddenly doesn't even know I exist, and him and overcoat man – whose name is Steve – just start walking down Bourke Street without even saying where they're going, and me and Sunny just have to follow like a couple of idiots. And I didn't even get to have my shower, which pisses me off something fierce.

They cross the road with car horns howling and me and Sunny nearly get hit, and they're acting like they own the town, and they're talking and I'm trying to listen, but the most I can work out is that Anton might know Steve from some place in North Melbourne.

But more than anything, I'm wondering just when in the world of fuck we're gonna score.

'We gonna get on it, or what?'

I think I must've said it pretty loud, or maybe even screamed it, because they both turn around and start laughing, almost like I'm a lunatic or something. Steve stops and puts his arm around me, which makes me shrink a bit inside.

He says he'll help me out.

'Just stick with me,' he says. 'I'll get us sorted.'

* * *

The problem with Steve 'getting us sorted', is that none of us has any money. I mean, Steve and Anton have a bit, but between both of them there's barely enough for anything. And I don't really want to turn a trick, if I can avoid it.

But Steve has an idea. He reckons me and Sunny would be good beggars, because of Sunny mostly. He reckons I can set up down on Swanston Street, just with a sign or something.

'Couple of hours,' he says, 'and we'll have more than we know what to do with.'

To be honest, I don't like begging. I've only ever done it once, when I was really stuck, and that was way before I was turning tricks. From what I remember, it wasn't much fun. I was never good at lying, and I reckon people could tell that I didn't really lose my purse, and I didn't really need to buy a bus ticket to Wodonga to see my mum, and she wasn't really sick.

In some ways, even though turning tricks can be completely gross, and sometimes pretty scary, it also feels pretty good. Not in a sexual way or nothing, but because I feel in control of things. Most of the time. It's kind of like my job, and I can decide how and when I earn money, you know? Almost like running my own business, I suppose. Like a profession.

Anton reckons that if I'm gonna keep doing it, I should go into a brothel or something, because it would be safer. But I like doing my own thing – I like being self-employed. I don't want someone telling me who and how I should fuck, and then keeping most of the money for themselves. And from what I know of those girls, it isn't any safer. If blokes pay enough, they basically get to do anything. Fisting, double-pen, scat, and some real sadistic stuff too. Most of what I do is pretty easy, once you get used to it.

Steve finds me a spot on the footpath between McDonald's and Off Ya Tree, which is a bong shop. He reckons being near McDonald's is good, because there will be heaps of people, and they'll have change from lunch or whatever. And he doesn't think anyone from Off Ya Tree will hassle me.

Anton nods like it's a good idea, but it seems like I have to do all the work.

'Don't worry, we'll keep an eye out,' he says. 'Just in case anyone gives you a hard time, or if the cops come.'

Steve gets some cardboard from a bin. He writes a note.

WHERE COLD. NEED A PLACE TO SLEEP FOR ME AND SONNY, IF U CAN SPARE SOME CHANGE.

'You spelled it wrong.'

'What?'

'Sunny.'

He looks at me sideways. 'Doesn't matter.'

I squat down on the footpath, cross my legs, and take off my beanie. The concrete is so fucking cold and my bum is freezing. There's just denim, cotton, and then my skin, and now I know why people use blankets when they beg.

I try not to add up after people drop their coins in, or watch too closely, because I don't want to look desperate. But it seems like it's going okay.

After a bit, a group of young guys walk past – high-school kids – and one yells out, 'Get a job!'

And I say, 'Eat a dick!'

So then his mate throws his empty Slurpee at me, except it isn't really empty, and I get Coke or something sweet and sticky all in my hair. They all laugh like it's the funniest thing ever.

I look around for Anton and Overcoat Steve, but they're nowhere. Sunny sits up and licks my face.

* * *

Some old lady comes up to me when it's almost dark. She bends down really slowly, like she's sore. She reads my sign, then puts a twenty-dollar note in my beanie.

It's pretty incredible, but it makes me feel bad. She smiles, but in a nice way – like she's trying especially hard to be respectful. She has gold-rimmed glasses and a black cloak and

I wonder if maybe she's a nun or something, but I don't get a chance to ask because Anton and Steve come back. Once she sees them both, standing there like freaks, the old lady moves away quickly, which is probably fair enough.

Anton's eyes are glassy and he has this woozy smile like he's been on the piss. He picks up my beanie, then holds up the twenty-dollar note to the light like he can't believe it's real.

'Jesus!' he says, and I can tell he's well pissed. Whatever cash they did have, they've blown it.

'Told ya, didn't I?' Steve has his overcoat done up right to his neck, and he looks like one of those ticket inspectors they have on the trams, except a junkie version.

'Let's go party, eh?'

He winks at me when he says it, and even though I'm dying for a hit, I wish it was just me and Anton. I wish it was just me and Anton and Sunny. I try to catch Anton's gaze, to show him what I'm feeling, but he's off somewhere else.

To be fair, it was Steve's idea that got us all that cash. But I still wish he wasn't there with his overcoat and his nose ring, and his hands deep in his pockets.

And with those eyes that glimmer darkly in the streetlight.

seven

I'm pretty shocked that Steve has a flat. Well, it isn't exactly his, as it turns out.

It's one of three on a block in Collingwood, all the same and in a row. His is at the front and the only one which is public housing, so he says. Inside, it's a bit of a mess, but not too bad. Although it stinks something terrible of smokes. Like old smoke, the stuff that gets stuck in the carpet and the furniture. There's something chemical too, I think. Or a bit like vinegar, but stronger.

'What's that smell?' I say.

He doesn't answer me.

There's heaps of footy posters plastered all along one wall.

'Collingwood fan?' Anton says. 'Never knew that.'

Steve takes off his overcoat. 'Nah, that's Mary.'

He has a faded black Bonds t-shirt underneath, and his arms are skinny and white. His left arm is scarred pretty bad in one spot, like he got burnt by boiling water or something. The skin there is all pink and rippled – it looks like an old scar, maybe from when he was a kid. And it suddenly makes me feel a bit sorry for him.

'Who's Mary?' I say.

'She lives here. But not right now.' He sits down on the couch.

'Where'd she go?'

'Psych ward. Had a flip out.'

Sunny curls up on the carpet like he's found a new home.

'We gonna get on it?' I say.

Steve smiles. 'Yep. And it's some good shit, you'll see.'

Anton has already taken his medicine, and he's pouring himself a drink from a bottle on a crappy-looking dresser with spirits all lined up. There's more pictures of Collingwood footballers above it, but in frames – almost like a shrine or something.

'Have as much as you like,' Steve says. 'It's all Mary's. I don't drink spirits.'

Anton smiles and raises his glass. 'Cheers to that.' He nods at me, 'You want one?'

'Nah.'

My arms are a bit shit at the moment, so I pull down my jeans and find a decent vein on the inside of my left thigh, right near the edge of my knickers. My veins are always hard to get at, which is generally a hassle.

When I stick it in, it hurts a bit, but not too bad.

Steve smiles at me, but he could be anyone, and I could be anywhere, because all there was and ever will be is *right there*. It's in my veins and it's coming on quick.

I close my eyes and... *Jesus*.

And I realise Steve's right. It is some really, really good shit.

* * *

I wake up with a jolt from a strange dream. It was something about some religion I'd joined, some sort of cult, and we were all in a camp together somewhere in the wilderness. I was trying to convince the other people that we were all being tricked, but no one would believe me.

There's music on. It's Cold Chisel's 'Flame Trees' and I've never liked their stuff. Steve is sitting on the floor, and he's got Sunny asleep next to him, and he's nodding along to the music like he thinks it was written especially for him, or something. My mouth is so dry and sticky I can barely open it.

'Where's Anton?' I say.

Steve is staring at the stereo and patting Sunny. 'Gone for a kip.'

I sit up straighter on the couch but my legs are stuck to it. It's an old vinyl thing and I wonder if it's Steve's or Mary's, or if they bought it together. I pull up my jeans.

'How long you been living here for?'

Steve smiles this sleepy grin.

'Hey,' I say, 'how long you been here for?'

His eyes are totally fucked and I figure he must've had another hit.

'Doesn't matter.'

'What?'

'Doesn't matter.' He coughs. 'It doesn't matter how long I've been here. How I got here matters more, don't ya reckon?'

I shrug.

He links his hands behind his head. 'Where we're going is even more important than that.'

I can tell Steve thinks he's a bit of a philosopher, or some shit. Some people get like that when they're on it. Usually blokes. Like they're suddenly a guru, or something.

I close my eyes and I think about what Steve said, even if he sounded like a bit of a dick. And I decide that it probably doesn't matter where we've been, or where we are, or even where we're going. But I don't say it out loud.

If I could decide where I was going, it would be somewhere warm, like Hervey Bay. I heard about Hervey Bay from this girl at the Salvos once. At first, I thought she said Harpy Bay, and she laughed at me like it was just the funniest thing ever. She was from Hervey Bay and she reckoned it was the most beautiful place in the world. She said the water was warm and it made you feel clean, and she couldn't wait to go back one day. But I don't really know what happened to her, or if she made it back to Hervey Bay.

I open my eyes and Steve is in the kitchen. I didn't even hear him get up.

'Tea?' he says.

That actually sounds pretty good.

I'd like a cup of tea, and I'd like one of those teddy bear biscuits. Or maybe even a milk-coffee one to dip, but that's probably asking too much.

He mustn't have a kettle or nothing, because he puts water in a saucepan on the stove. The stove is one of those old electric ones with the coils, and it's probably gonna take forever. I wonder how he knows Anton. They were talking about a place in North Melbourne, and I remember Anton saying once how he stayed at a halfway house round there just after he got out. It was only for a few days, because he really hated it.

Maybe they knew each other before that. Anton doesn't make friends very easy, though. To be honest, I'm not even sure if Steve actually is his friend, but he seems like something close to it.

He stands in the kitchen with his back against the fridge, like he's watching and waiting for the water, but I can tell he's posing a bit, like he thinks he's pretty good or something. Men are hopeless at shit like that – always so obvious.

'So,' he says, 'how long you been in the park?'

I shrug. 'Couple of years. Maybe less.'

'Anton?'

'Same.'

'Been inside?'

'Me?'

'Yeah.'

'Nah. You?'

He smiles. 'How do you like it?'

'What?'

'Your tea.'

I can hear morning birds outside. I look past Steve, out the window above the sink, and the sky is mostly black, but starting to get that deep blue near the horizon, which means the sun isn't far away.

'How do you know each other?' I say.

He crosses his arms, but doesn't answer. He looks at the pot, which is starting to simmer and fizz.

'Was it the place in North Melbourne?'

He cuts his eyes to me. 'How do you know about that?'

'Heard you talking.'

'When?'

'Dunno. When we first met up?'

He goes quiet for a bit.

And I say, 'So?'

'So what?'

'Is that how you know each other?'

'Yeah,' he says, 'we knew each other. I used to work there.' I can tell he doesn't want to talk much more about it. And I figure me and Anton best be going after I have my tea, partly because I'm a bit worried about our stuff back at the park, but also because I don't think there's any gear left.

So it'll be just me and Steve sitting around until Anton wakes up, and I don't want Steve to try anything. He isn't bad looking or nothing, but I'm not really up for it. If he pays, maybe, but I figure he'd just be paying with the cash I made anyway.

'Better head soon,' I say.

He's making the tea carefully, tipping the steaming water slowly into two white mugs. And I wonder if hot water was what made the burn on his arm. He doesn't look up.

'How about another hit instead?'

eight

It wasn't like there was a discussion about it. Or maybe there was, but I wasn't asked. Maybe Anton and Steve decided while I was asleep. Or maybe they decided while they were out drinking, and I was begging. I don't really know.

But me and Anton are gonna crash at Steve's for a while.

'Till Mary comes back,' Anton says.

Steve scratches at the scar on his arm. Makes me squirm inside. 'Could be a long time,' he says. 'Well, as long as you want to hang around, anyway.'

Steve reckons the rent comes straight out of her dole, so we don't need to worry.

I guess you'd think I'd jump at the chance of having a roof over our heads. But I've kind of gotten used to being in the park. And the spot we've got, under the back of the grandstand, is pretty much prime real estate as far as it goes. It's under cover and mostly out of the wind, so if you leave it for too long you can be guaranteed someone else will have taken it. Which means, by the time we leave Steve and Mary's, we'll probably have to move to a new spot.

Some people might wonder why we wouldn't just go into a homeless shelter instead. But people who wonder about that have never stayed in a shelter, I don't reckon. Plus, I've got Sunny to think of.

Staying here is what Anton wants, I suppose, to get a flat

and all that. Could be like a practice run. Still, I feel a bit funny about the idea. I'm used to it just being me, Anton and Sunny. In some ways, Steve actually seems pretty nice. But there's something that makes me a bit uncomfortable. It isn't something I can put a name to, or anything I can really explain, not exactly. But it kind of reminds me of this schoolteacher I once had – it's the same kind of feeling.

I got sick this one time on school camp. I'd been kicked out of my old school and the camp was in the first week of the new one. It was at a lake, which was almost dry and pretty awful, and because I didn't know anyone it was doubly shitful. Anyway, it was a three-night deal, and on the second night I got sick, spewing up and that. I think it was probably from some sausages that weren't cooked properly, so I had to go lie down in my cabin while everyone else watched a movie about some pig who could talk. It was like this special video night, which they were all excited about.

So I was lying in the cabin, trying not to think about spewing again, and the room was spinning a bit, and then there was this soft knocking at the door.

He came in all slow and very quiet. I can't remember his name now, but he was tall – I remember that. And he had one of those shirts like Steve Irwin used to wear, like he thought he was on safari or something, just because he was on school camp. Bit of a dick.

He stood inside the doorway.

'How are you feeling?'

Even though I told him I was okay, that I was feeling better, he shut the door behind him and sat on the bed. After a bit, he started stroking my hair.

The skin on his neck was bright red and I could smell aftershave and sweat all mixed together, and I knew there was something weird about the whole situation. I mean, I was only twelve, but I'd seen enough to know when people were weirdos, and when they were planning something sexual.

It was pretty horrible.

To be fair, I don't think Steve is a pedo or anything. I just mean there's something not right. Like there's a gap between what he says and what he's thinking. The words roll off all smooth, but it's like there's something completely different going on underneath.

But Anton, he seems pretty cool with the whole deal. So I don't think I'll say anything to him about it. Not yet.

* * *

Steve is making coffee and toast. It's already after lunch, I think, and we've slept right through the morning.

It's comfy on the couch, and Sunny is asleep on the floor in front of me, almost like he's been living here all his life. Sunny's like that – he can just about lie down anywhere and feel like he's at home. I originally got him from this old bloke who slept at the park sometimes – his name was Kevin. He kept to himself and he only had one eye, so people called him Kevin With One Eye, because there was another bloke named Kevin who used to stay there too.

I always thought it would have been better to call him One-eyed Kevin, but I suppose he got used to the other name. I think he'd had a stroke or something, because you could hardly understand a word he said.

Anyway, one night he just died in his sleeping bag, with Sunny right there next to him. Sunny didn't move from his side, even though Kevin was well and truly dead, and he surely must've known. The police and ambulance came next morning, and one of the coppers asked me if I knew whose dog it was.

'He's mine,' I said.

I knew if they took him, he'd almost definitely get put down. That didn't seem fair on him. Or Kevin.

The copper probably twigged that I was lying, because he asked what his name was, and I said it was Sunny because – like I said – it was sunny that morning, and it was the first thing that came into my head. I've never known what his real name is.

Sometimes, me and Anton try to guess his real name. Like, we'll say different names and see if he reacts. But we still haven't got it right, not yet.

It's funny with dogs. I mean, the connection you have with them. Anton says that it goes back to when they were wolves and people lived in caves. He said the wolves used to come to get food and warmth, and that's how they became close to people. He said the cavemen were happy to have them, because they made excellent guards and kept the other cavemen away.

His theory was the cavemen didn't train the wolves – he reckoned the wolves trained the cavemen, because they got food and shelter out of the whole deal, and didn't have to do very much. It makes a bit of sense, if you think about it.

Steve gets some raspberry jam and margarine from the fridge, like he's laying it all out a bit. Like he's trying to make a good impression. Be a good host, as they say.

The coffee is shithouse, and the milk curdles a bit like it might be off. But the toast is nice. I feel a lot better after eating something, especially something sweet like jam, and Anton puts on the TV like he's making himself at home. It's one of those panel shows with a bunch of people talking crap.

Then Steve says, 'Maybe you should go out begging again.'

I swallow my toast down, but a bit catches in my throat. 'Why?'

'You did really well yesterday.'

I look at Anton, because I hope he'll see it in my eyes, and then say we've got other plans or something. But he just keeps watching the TV until the ads come on.

Then he says, 'Yeah, might be an idea. Tide us over till the dole comes through, you know?' He doesn't look at me when he says it, but starts flicking through the channels. He finally looks up, catches my gaze. 'Only if you want to, though.'

'What about Centrelink?' I say, because it's the first thing that comes into my head.

He coughs. 'What about it?'

'Don't you want to go back? About the flat, I mean.'

Steve shoots me a look. 'What flat?'

'Nothing. I mean, there's no flat,' I say. 'But we wanna get on the waiting list.'

Anton changes the channel and it looks like *The Bill* is on, which one of my fosters used to watch all the time. There were about a million episodes and they were always showing old repeats, and the cops were all nice, which isn't like in real life.

'Yeah,' Anton says, 'I do want to go back. Eventually. But me and Steve have some things to do first.'

I wonder what, but decide not to ask.

'Maybe you should get our stuff then,' I say. 'From the park, before it gets nicked.'

Anton leans back on the couch and stretches. 'I'll try,' he says. 'Otherwise we'll both go. After you finish.'

* * *

It's pretty cold again, but Steve has given me a blanket this time, so at least I've got something to sit on. I forgot to bring the sign though, so I have to write a new one.

I get some cardboard from out of a bin – the lid of a shoebox, which is just perfect. I go into a newsagent and have to queue up for a bit, which makes me nervous because I've had to leave Sunny outside.

The shop owner is some old Indian guy. Eyes me all suspicious.

'Can I borrow a pen?'

Shakes his head. 'No, sorry.'

'Just for a minute.' I hold up the cardboard.

'No, no. Sorry.'

Pisses me off a bit, but I keep quiet.

I go to a 7-Eleven instead and some young Chinese guy is

behind the counter. He has thick, black-rimmed glasses and his eyes are a bit googly, but he smiles all friendly and gives me a pen.

'You keep it,' he says, which is pretty nice.

'Thanks very much,' I say.

My handwriting was never great, but I'm okay at spelling –

PLEASE CAN YOU SPARE SOME CHANGE FOR ME AND MY DOG, SO WE CAN STAY SOMEWHERE WARM TONIGHT.

I know it isn't very creative, but I figure bringing Sunny into the equation is a good idea. It worked last time.

People feel more sorry for dogs and animals than other people, I reckon. It's because they figure it's not really the dog's fault they're in that situation. Same with little kids, I suppose. And especially babies. It's never their fault they have shithouse parents – just bad luck. A lot of things like that just come down to luck, when you think about it.

I go to the same spot because it went okay last time. And it's all going pretty well, no one hassling me or anything. People are putting money in without really reading the sign, and I reckon Sunny has a lot to do with that. He's just sleeping and chilling out – a good gig for him really, boring as hell for me though.

'You want something to eat?'

I look up and it's some old do-gooder in a white shirt, black pants and really shiny shoes. It'd be better if he gave me some money, but seems a bit rude to say it.

'Thanks,' I say. 'Maybe a cheeseburger? From Maccas? And a hot apple pie?'

That probably seems greedy, but you never know unless you ask.

He smiles, disappears inside. He's gone for ages, and I wonder if he's coming back. But then he returns, passes the brown paper bag to me without a word.

'Thanks,' I say. 'Really nice of you.'

He smiles, but stays there. And I realise he's going to watch me eat, which is a bit weird. It's making me uncomfortable, so I wolf it down as quick as I can. I even give the last bit of the burger to Sunny.

As soon as I'm done, he starts. 'Have you heard the good news?'

'What?'

'The good news.'

'Good news about what?'

He claps his hands together. 'My child! The good news about the Lord Our Saviour, Jesus Christ!'

Honestly, I should have seen it coming.

I'm polite for a while, seeing how he got me the food, but he gets on my nerves pretty quick. He keeps talking about *the righteous path* and *those who stray* and he's getting himself all worked up. Apart from anything else, he's bad for business.

'Look,' I say, 'thanks so much for the food, I appreciate it. But I'm not into any of that.'

'Not into it?'

'Nah.'

'My child, you may not be *into it*, but God is *into you*!'

He's really on a roll. I pack up my blanket and my sign. Loop the rope around Sunny's neck.

'What are you doing?' he says.

'Have to go.'

'I'll come with you!'

'No thanks.'

I take Sunny by the rope and walk quickly up the street. He follows me for a bit, but gives up once I get round the corner.

Look, I'm not ungrateful or anything – the food was nice, the apple pie especially – but it seems like everything comes with strings attached. With some people, anyway. Like, they can't just do you a favour without expecting something in return, you know?

I wait for a bit, just to make sure he's not still hanging

around. Once I'm certain, I go back round the corner to the spot between Off Ya Tree and McDonald's, because it had been going okay till he showed up.

By the way, you might think the Off Ya Tree customers would be generous because they're stoners or whatever, but I was doing way better out of the McDonald's customers. More from old people than teenagers, I think. But maybe it just depends on the day.

After a little while, one of the staff from McDonald's comes out.

'Hello,' he says. I can see from his badge that his name is Simon and he's the Assistant Manager. Couldn't be more than twenty – all braces and bad skin. Kind of cute.

'Hey,' I say.

'Want some water?'

'Water?'

'For the dog.'

I nod. 'Thanks, Simon.'

He gives Sunny a pat. 'What's his name?'

'Sunny.'

He smiles. 'Sweet. Back in a tick then.'

He returns with a little plastic container and Sunny slurps it up like crazy. I wonder if Simon always wanted to be Assistant Manager at McDonald's. Like, if that was his dream when he was a little kid. I doubt it. Seems pretty happy all the same.

'If you need anything,' he says, 'just give me a shout.'

He's pretty nice.

I'm surprised the people who work at Off Ya Tree aren't so nice. They kind of ignore me, like they're too cool or something. Or maybe they think I'm bad for business, like I'm an advertisement for where it could all end up. Like if there was a 'before and after' photo, I'm the 'after'.

You get a lot of time to think, sitting out begging, which isn't always a good thing. I wish I had a book or a magazine or something, just to pass the time. I've never been much of a reader, but there was one book I liked at one of the high schools I was at. It was an old book called *Summer of the Seventeenth Doll*. I think it was originally a play, so some of the smarter kids got parts to read out in class.

It was a good story, and it was set in Melbourne too. I can't remember exactly what happens, but it was about some farm workers from Queensland who come to the city every year. I remember the teacher saying it was mostly about how things always change, even if we don't want them to.

I wonder what Anton is doing with Steve that's so important. Probably nothing. It pisses me off that it's up to me to get the money, while they just dick around.

Maybe they aren't just dicking around though, maybe they're actually doing something important. I can't imagine what, and it makes me worry a bit, because me and Anton always do pretty much everything together. I've just gotten used to him being around, I suppose. Him and Sunny.

Sunny is like magic. He can almost make you forget about anything when he puts his head up on your leg. He's always warm and he smells like home, more than anything in the world. It might sound a bit kooky, but I really think Sunny understands and loves me, more than anyone. He probably loved old Kevin With One Eye too, but he's dead.

Sunny can tell what I'm feeling, even if I don't say a word. That's pretty amazing if you think about it. Like, Sunny can tell when I'm starting to get a bit strung out, even if I'm not showing it on the outside yet. It's like he can feel the same thing, think the same thoughts. Hear the same things I can hear.

He moves closer to me on the blanket. Sighs like he's just so tired of all this, which is probably fair enough. And then I see the shiny black shoes back in front of me.

I wonder why in the world of fuck has the Christian decided to come back? But when I look up, it isn't him after all.

It's a copper.

nine

Good thing is, I know this copper. It's Dirty Doug.

'Well then.' He smiles. 'New line of work?'

'Yep, a promotion.'

He turns to his partner, Constable Martinovic – I see that on her badge. He says something to her out the side of his mouth, but loud enough so I can hear.

'Harmless.'

She's barely in her twenties I reckon, but has already perfected that 'no-face' expression that coppers get, like they give you nothing of what they're thinking or feeling. Me and Anton call it 'no-face', because it was the name of this character from a Jap cartoon movie we saw once at Nova.

Sometimes, if it's the middle of the day, the Cinema Nova people pretend not to see us sneak in. I don't know if it's because they're scared, or because of how we look, or if they're just being nice. But I like to think it's because they're nice.

But we haven't done that in ages. Since I got Sunny, we haven't gone to the movies so much. Apart from that convent one.

Dirty Doug squats in front of me. 'You're not supposed to be begging, you know.'

I shrug. I've never known why he's called Dirty Doug. Maybe I should have asked, but it's been way too long now. It'd be awkward.

Sunny gets up and leans in for a lick.

'Remembers you,' I say.

'Could he forget this face?'

Dirty Doug is right about that, because he has this big red birthmark over one side of his face. He told me once that it used to be called a port-wine stain, back when he was a kid, but they aren't allowed to use that name anymore, because it isn't 'politically correct', whatever that means. He said it had another name now, and he told me what it was, but all I can ever remember is port-wine stain, because that's pretty much exactly what it looks like. Like someone spilled red wine on his skin, and they tried to clean it, but it never came off.

'How's Anton? You two still a couple?'

'Never were,' I say. 'Why, you keen?'

He laughs and glances back at his partner. She gives this tight little smile, like she thinks it's something she should do, even if she doesn't feel like it.

I know Dirty Doug because he's seen me on the street heaps of times. He even caught me turning a trick once with some fat Turkish bloke in a laneway. Just a hand job. He's never charged me with nothing, but always gives my clients a pretty hard time.

That's what he calls them, 'clients'. And he reckons I should be more careful, because he says clients who don't use brothels usually have a reason, and it isn't a good one. He's probably right about that.

But he doesn't talk about any of that in front of Constable Martinovic. And I'm glad.

'So just a social visit?' I say.

'We got a complaint,' he says.

'The Christian?'

'Who?'

'Doesn't matter.'

He nods towards Off Ya Tree, then rolls his eyes. 'Can you believe it?'

That's the thing, even though coppers aren't always nice

and friendly like the ones on *The Bill*, some are actually all right.

I almost tell him my theory about me being bad advertising – the 'before and after' thing – but think better of it.

'Still staying in the park?' he says.

'Nah, someone's place for a bit.'

'That's good.'

'Yeah, maybe.'

He stands up, but groans on the way like his knees are sore. Like he's older than he looks. 'Well, best you get moving from here though.'

'Yeah.'

'Lesser of two evils, I s'pose.' He says it sort of to himself, but I think I know what he means.

He leans back down and gives Sunny a pat.

'Still on it?'

He says it without looking at me, with his eyes on Sunny like he already knows the answer. And I wonder why he bothered asking then.

'Nah,' I say. 'This is all just recreation. A hobby, you know? How I pass the time. Socialising.'

He reaches inside my beanie and lifts out a handful of gold coins.

'Doing all right?' he says.

'Not bad.'

Thing is, I'd already added up the money round the corner, while I was waiting for the Christian to rack off. With the additional since, I had plenty.

I suddenly wonder if maybe I should go score on my own, because I'll still have enough left so Anton and Steve won't know, and then I can have an extra hit later.

And just when I'm thinking about this, Steve turns up.

He stops behind Dirty Doug and Constable Martinovic. He hesitates, like he doesn't want to be seen. Shoots me a look, then walks slowly up the street for a bit, acting like he doesn't know me, but glancing back once, twice, then a third time, before stopping at the corner.

It's almost like he could read my mind or something, like he knew I was planning to use some of the cash for myself.

I wonder why Anton hasn't come and why it's just Steve. I think he's waiting for the coppers to go, which is probably fair enough. But then Dirty Doug notices me looking up the street, follows my gaze.

'Know him?' he says.

I loop the rope around Sunny's neck. 'Who?'

'Don't play smart.'

'Dunno what you're talking about.'

'Giving you trouble?'

'Honest, don't know who you mean, officer.'

I glance up the street and Steve is gone. A ghost. Like he was never there in the first place.

Constable Martinovic's radio crackles to life, but I can't hear what it's about. She squints and listens in.

'Better head,' she says.

Dirty Doug nods, but keeps his eyes on me. 'Be careful, you know? Company you keep.'

It's a pretty strange thing to say, especially because he knows my usual line of work. I mean, I'm always as careful as I can be, but weirdos go with the territory.

Still, I know who he's actually talking about, even if he doesn't say it.

* * *

Steve holds Sunny while I pack up.

'Where's Anton?' I say.

'Busy. I was worried you might get lost.'

'Lost?'

'On the way to the flat.'

I tie up the money in my beanie, place it on the blanket, then roll it up. Steve picks up my sign. Smiles.

'Partly true,' he says. 'That makes the best lies.'

'What do you mean?'

'If they've got a bit of truth in them. A half-truth, I think they call it.'

'Right.'

'Want a coffee, or something?'

I'm guessing Steve might feel a bit guilty about me being out there all day on my own. Still, it's a pretty good offer.

I head for one of the fast-food joints with the seats outside, but Steve says, 'Tourist trap,' and takes me to Brunetti's instead. It's in the City Square over the road, and the staff wear little black vests and bow-ties, which are kind of ridiculous.

He gets me a cappuccino, which is my favourite, and he uses his own money, instead of the money I'd just made. The coffee is delicious, even if they forgot to put the chocolate on top.

He waits till I've drunk my coffee to ask.

'How much then?'

I don't know exactly, even though I've done a rough count.

'About seventy?'

He raises his eyebrows like he's pretty impressed. It was lucky I didn't go off and score on my own. I'd probably feel pretty bad about it now, especially seeing how nice he's being.

It's almost dusk and I can feel the chill on my skin, but it's good to sit and watch the people go past. They're all heading for Flinders Street Station, like some long river of dark suits – going from their office, or their shop, or whatever, to catch a train to take them home to eat and sleep, and do it all again tomorrow, and maybe the same thing every day forever.

I haven't got anything against those people, but it's just never gonna be my life. And I know some of those people probably feel sorry for me, or scared, or maybe worse. They wouldn't want my life, I know that – and I probably wouldn't want theirs.

Still, it would be better to be in the middle, I think – with a life somewhere between mine and theirs. But I don't really know what that would look like, or if it could even happen.

I put my cup under the table and Sunny licks the froth left inside. He looks up at me with these dark shiny eyes, like it's the nicest thing anyone has ever done for him in his life.

'Another coffee?' Steve says. 'Cake?'

'Cake might be nice.'

It's funny with people – you can think one thing on one day, then something completely different the next.

Sitting out at Brunetti's with Steve, I'd have to admit I'm in a pretty good mood. I want to get on it something fierce, but I know we've got money and it's definitely gonna happen, which is always a good feeling.

The anticipation can be really great. Not as good as the real deal, but pretty sweet all the same.

* * *

On the way back to the flat, I ask him.

'What did you and Anton do all day?'

He smiles and says, 'Not much,' then snorts to himself, which is kind of weird. I can tell he tried to stifle it. 'Just kept busy, you know.'

Collins Street is steep, and it's getting cold, and I'm looking forward to seeing Anton. He'll be pretty happy with how well I've done.

Steve walks really quick and I have trouble keeping up, but Sunny is enjoying the pace. Steve is one of those blokes who likes to cross roads wherever he wants, without the lights or anything, which isn't what normal people do. I guess that's probably the point.

Anton does it sometimes too, except I tell him off about it because we've got Sunny and it's dangerous. I don't feel like I can say something like that to Steve, though. I don't know him well enough, or how he might react.

'What did those coppers say?'

He says it without looking back at me, and it was hard to hear him because a tram was going past, but I caught it all the same.

'Nothing,' I say, a bit too loud. 'Just that I was begging and it was illegal and all that.'

He shoots this sharp look at me.

'You looked pretty chummy with that bloke, though.'

'Who?'

'With the weird face.'

'Nah,' I say. 'He's just a bit of a sleaze.'

I feel bad saying that about Dirty Doug, especially when it isn't true. But I can tell being friendly with a copper isn't gonna do me any favours with Steve.

I do wonder what Dirty Doug knows about Steve, but I figure it's probably just about him being on the gear. Dirty Doug is always banging on about how I should get into a rehab program, or something. And I always tell him I've got it under control, which is mostly true.

It's nice he gives a shit, I suppose.

ten

The flat is close to the housing commission towers in Collingwood, so it isn't the best area or anything. It's that low part, down towards Hoddle Street. Hoddle Street is about ten lanes wide and just horrible – you can actually hear all the cars and trucks as clear as anything, even though it's a few streets away.

It makes me think of that guy and how he went crazy that time. I can't remember how many people he killed, but it was a lot. It happened years ago, but Anton told me all about it. He reckoned the guy did it because he was bullied in the army, or something like that.

It was a strange place to do it. I mean, it's like a freeway almost. You'd expect the Bourke Street Mall, or a shopping centre, or maybe a school, if you were going to do something crazy like that. But Hoddle Street was a weird choice.

Anton says that no one talks about him much nowadays, especially since that albino in Tasmania killed heaps more people. It's like he's pretty much forgotten – everyone always moves on pretty quick like that. Anton reckons people have got 'short memories', and that's probably true.

But anyway, like I was saying, the flat is in a pretty crappy spot. I know it probably sounds a bit rich to be complaining when I normally sleep in a park. But just because I don't have a house, doesn't mean I've got no taste.

Princes Park is a great spot. It's green, pretty close to the city, and there are beautiful streets all around with old terrace houses and some places which are nearly like mansions. I know me and Anton and Sunny could never live in any of those houses, but we get to live in the same suburb, and just across the road, which is almost as good.

But Steve and Mary's flat is in a dead zone. The area probably used to be full of factories and all that, which is probably why they put the commission houses there. It's close enough to the city, but there's not much public transport apart from buses, and no one likes to take buses very much. It doesn't make much difference to me though, because I have to walk everywhere with Sunny anyway.

By the time we get back, it's completely dark. Anton isn't home, which is a bit of a surprise. But I'm also a bit surprised by what's in the lounge room, and I can see what Steve meant when he said they'd been busy.

There are two flat-screen TVs, three laptop computers, and a bunch of other electronic stuff, which might be for computer games or something.

'Where did all this—?'

'Anton's been a good help,' Steve says. 'Really good.'

I'm a bit shocked. I mean, Anton is no saint or nothing, but we'd never even talked about doing burgs, or anything like that. I'm not into that sort of thing, and it can be pretty dangerous. Plus, for Anton, with his record, he'll end up back in jail for sure. If he gets caught.

'Where is he?' I say.

Steve picks up one of the laptops. He types on the keyboard, even though it's not on. 'Pretty schmick, eh? Student house – perfect. We'll head back there in a few months, once they get their insurance.'

'Where's Anton?'

Steve's eyes go a bit dark. He lets out a tired sigh, puts the laptop down on the floor.

'How the fuck should I know? I had to go pick you up, remember?'

There's a knock at the door.

Steve says, 'That'll be him,' then yells out, 'It's open!'

Makes me jump.

Anton comes in slow and he looks at me a bit sheepish, but with a bit of a smirk underneath. He's wearing a navy blue woollen jacket, which I've never seen before, and I wonder if Steve loaned it to him, or if he nicked it from one of the students.

'Look at you,' Steve says. 'Like a rat with a gold tooth.'

Anton squeezes my arm as he passes. 'Just this once, yeah? Give us a bit of a buffer.'

A buffer. I suppose he means some extra cash, just in case we need it down the track.

Steve slaps Anton on the back. 'Was just showing off some of our hard work,' he says. 'She doesn't seem too impressed, but.'

'It's not that,' I say. 'Just if the coppers—'

'Don't worry about the pigs,' Steve says. 'I know what I'm doin.'

Anton picks up what looks like a controller for one of those game things. A Nintendo, or whatever.

'If we save some of the cash,' he says, 'it'll help when we get our own place. You know?'

'What about our stuff?'

'What?'

'At the park. We were gonna go get it, remember?'

He doesn't answer for a bit. Coughs. 'Tomorrow,' he says.

One day might be okay, but any longer and people will start to pick through our stuff. It's not like they want to steal, but they just assume you're not coming back, or that maybe something has happened.

Steve gets himself a beer. 'So, you got it?'

Anton reaches into the back pocket of his jeans. 'Yeah,

managed to offload the phones. He reckons he can move the TVs as well, so we're all set.'

He pulls out a large baggie, which has some smaller baggies inside. I can see the powder and I know he's got me sorted. And suddenly, our stuff at the park doesn't matter so much.

It's funny how it makes everything else just fall away like that – that's one of the great things about it. It gives you focus, you know? It's like all those other thoughts and worries just disappear so quickly, and all you can think about is how you're gonna feel.

Tomorrow doesn't matter so much. Or the next day. Or even the day after that.

* * *

I'm in a thick pumpkin soup or something, like everything is so heavy and sweet. Warm and slow.

It's fucking beautiful really. In its way.

We're sitting on the floor and I'm patting Sunny. I have to remember to feed him, once I don't feel so heavy.

Anton is DJ because he's able to keep it together. He's playing some old shit, Velvet Underground. It's all about waiting for my man, which Steve thinks is pretty funny.

He reckons Anton should have a hit.

'Magic, this stuff.'

He's right about that, but I know what Anton will say.

'Nah, I'm good.'

Steve shrugs. 'Your loss.'

He turns and smiles at me, and it's kind of nice for once to have someone feeling the same thing I am.

Like I said, Anton won't ever shoot up. On the pills, he can keep things more under control. He knows how much he's taking and all that. It's not like with smack, where you don't know how strong it is, or anything about it really.

I think those are probably his reasons, but I don't think he's ever actually explained it. Not completely.

* * *

Sunny is asleep. I'm patting him right down the middle of his back, which I think he likes. He's snoring.

'I love this song,' Steve says.

It's 'All Tomorrow's Parties', which has already been on about three times. It's one of those songs I've always found depressing, but don't really know why.

Steve stands up and starts doing this weird dance on his own, spinning slowly like some kind of loopy hippy, with his arms out to the side and his eyes closed like he's in a dream.

I look over and Anton is asleep.

It's just me and Steve and Sunny.

Steve and Sunny and me.

In the soup.

eleven

I wake up and it feels like it's pretty early. I'm hot from sleeping in a bed with a doona, which I'm not really used to. I sit up, strip off my t-shirt, then lay back down.

Soft light filters in from around the blind, and I stay there for a while and listen. The house is quiet and I can hear the hum of Hoddle Street and I wonder what it's like for the people driving to work, or wherever they're going. I wonder if they're happy.

I remember in school I had this teacher who was the careers adviser as well. She reckoned I could become a nurse or something. She said it would be a 'good option' because there were always jobs for nurses, and I wondered if that was why she became a teacher too. I didn't say it, though.

Her name was Miss Everleigh and she had brown hair and coloured stockings, and she pashed a year nine boy at a party once. She lost her job after that, but came back again a year later. It probably wasn't a very good school, I don't think.

I wasn't into school that much anyway. Some of my fosters were all about studying, but I don't think they really understood how it works. I mean, once you fall behind by a certain amount, there's really not much point anymore. And because I'd been moved around so much, and got kicked out of a few places, I could never really follow what was being taught. I think some of my fosters thought they would be my saviour or something, especially the Christian ones. The Christian ones were always the worst about school. Worst about everything, really.

Some fosters didn't give much of a shit about school, or even if I went. They were more interested in other stuff. I don't like to think about that too much. What's the point, right?

I've been given the spare room – that's what Steve calls it – but I can tell it's actually Mary's room, because her stuff is still on the floor. There's clothes and shoes and things like that, and I wonder why she didn't take any of it with her.

I sit up on the edge of the bed. I think for a minute about maybe wearing her clothes, because mine are pretty rank, and I don't feel like putting them back on again. I pick up a pair of jeans, which are black Levi's, but they look a bit too small. Not that I'm fat or anything, but Mary must be tiny, especially around the waist. There's a couple of t-shirts that look all right, but it's probably a pretty shithouse thing to do. I mean, she's sick and in a psych ward. If it was me, I wouldn't want anyone wearing my clothes. I'd really flip out, which is probably even more likely if I'd been in the loony bin.

Besides, there's always the chance she might come back unannounced, which could be pretty awkward. And if she sees me in her clothes, you could multiply that by a thousand. Basically, I don't want any trouble. And it's probably bad enough that I've been sleeping in her bed. Like Goldilocks, or something.

I go out to the lounge and it stinks bad of cigarettes. And I notice that chemical smell again, stronger than before. It's like I can taste it more than I can smell it. Like vinegar, but more meaty now too. Almost like dog food, somewhere underneath it.

Anton is asleep on the couch. He has his face fully buried in the cushion and there's a trail of drool on it. He looks kind of cute, like a little boy who's gotten really tired watching TV, or something. I keep the blinds down so I don't wake him.

The door to Steve's bedroom is shut, so I figure he's probably still asleep too.

Sunny is awake and has done a shit in front of the TV, which is probably mixing in with the stink and only making it worse. That must be the meaty smell. I find a plastic bag under the sink and scoop it up, and it leaves a bit of a smear on the carpet, but not so much anyone would notice. I don't tell him off for it, because it isn't his fault he can't get outside or anything.

I make some toast as quietly as I can. The bread is pretty stale, but it's usually fine once you toast it. I have the last of the raspberry jam and it's lovely and sweet. I boil water for some coffee. Even though Steve and Mary's coffee is crap, it's better than nothing.

I find a half-empty jar of Vegemite in the fridge, which is weird because I think it's usually kept in the cupboard. I make Anton some toast – nice way to wake him, I reckon.

* * *

It's a long walk to the park, but it isn't too cold. Must be Saturday, because there's lots of kids around. Saturday is like a sports day or something, because there are always kids in soccer gear and that sort of thing, getting into cars and that.

The kids always look pretty happy, like it's probably their favourite thing to be doing. I suppose it's nice for them to be with their parents, and they're happy their parents come watch them play. Like, if their team wins, it'll make them proud or something.

And maybe their parents are proud if they win, but I'm not sure why. I mean, what does it really prove about anything? Sport, I mean.

Most of the parents look pretty happy too, which annoys me a bit. But a few don't, like there are a million better things to do on a Saturday, which is probably true.

It's not something I'd ever want to be doing. If I had kids,

I mean. If I had kids, I reckon I'd be most proud if they were good people, you know? Like, if they had friends and were nice to other kids at school or whatever. Not so much about sport.

To be fair, I've never been into sport – don't really see the point. Anton reckons he used to play footy back in the town where he's from. But he gave it up once he started shearing, mainly because he didn't have the time, and then the shearing fucked his back up anyway.

It's good to be out walking with Anton again. Just me and him and Sunny. I mean, Steve has been good to us and everything, and it's nice to have a place to sleep, but I miss being outside in the fresh air. And when you're walking, it's easier to talk about things. The things on my mind.

'What do you reckon that smell is?'

Anton eyes me. 'What smell?'

'In the flat.'

He frowns. 'Haven't really noticed.'

'You're joking, right? That chemical smell.'

A fire truck comes screaming up the street, sirens blaring. Anton waits until it's passed.

'Oh yeah, maybe a bit. Like detergent?'

'More like vinegar. Or dog food. Dunno... it's something though.'

Anton shrugs. 'Could be cooking.'

'What? Meth?'

'Maybe. Doing it in his room.'

I've never smelled it being cooked before, but I'd heard it was rank. Would make a bit of sense, I suppose. Still, I wonder why Steve hasn't mentioned it. Must want it all for himself.

We have to cross Alexandra Parade, so I bring Sunny in on a shorter rope.

'For money, you think?'

Anton looks at me. 'What else?'

'I suppose. I mean, doesn't seem to be using it.'

Anton shrugs. 'Could be from ages ago – the smell, I mean.

The stink can stay around for months. Besides, he's mostly doing burgs now.'

The light goes green and we cross quickly. If you get caught halfway on Alexandra Parade, you're stuck there for ages.

'Why'd you do it?' I say.

'Do what?'

'The burg.'

Anton shakes his head. 'It was Steve's idea. For me to come, I mean. Extra set of hands.'

'Where was it?'

'Clifton Hill, I think. Or Fitzroy North? Around there somewhere. Can never tell the difference.'

There are a few dogs up ahead outside a café, so I pull Sunny in tighter. It isn't like he's aggressive or anything, but people get the wrong idea sometimes, just because of how he looks. I mean, some people even cross the street when they see us coming. People don't realise he's just a massive sook.

'You gonna do it again?'

He shrugs. 'Dunno. I mean, like I was saying, it could be good to get us some money and that. For the flat, you know? For us.'

It's nice to hear him talk about 'us'. Even if the flat is a bit of a pipedream.

I think to tell him to be careful with the burgs, because he could end up in jail again. And I want to ask him about when we might leave the flat, and go back to the park.

But then the sun breaks through the clouds – it's warm, he looks happy, and I don't want to be a downer.

* * *

It's not really a surprise. I half-expected it. Still, it pisses me off.

Most of our stuff is gone, even the sleeping bags and the umbrella I'd nicked from a hotel foyer in the city. It was a beauty, a big black one with Park Hyatt in gold letters, which

Anton always thought was hilarious. My bag is still there and some of my clothes, but someone has gone through it, and most of my stuff is out on the ground and a bit wet.

Anton's bag is gone, but he doesn't seem too worried. He lights a smoke.

'It's all right,' he says. 'We can offload some of the gear and get new clothes. Probably about time anyway.'

There are a few of the long-termers still asleep in their sleeping bags. 'Should we ask?'

I figure they might know who took our stuff, or at least we can see if they have it, which is probably more likely.

'Nah,' he says. 'Just forget it. Probably high-school kids.'

A lot of high-school kids hang out at the park after school, or wag there sometimes. They're usually pretty harmless. I even turned a few tricks with a couple of the older boys, which was pretty good. They were polite, awkward, and would usually blow their load in a heartbeat. Easy money.

'Anyway,' he says, 'these blokes have it hard enough.'

That's the thing. Anton has never really seen himself as being like the others. Homeless – I don't think I've ever heard him even say the word. To be fair, he looks different from most of the blokes sleeping rough. Maybe that's part of why he thinks the whole thing on the street is just temporary, because he's not much like the others.

But he carries himself different too, if that makes sense. Has a different outlook. It's like this is only ever going to be a short-term thing, being on the streets, and eventually he'll get out of it. He just has that belief and it's enough to pull him through.

He's good like that, kind of calm and level-headed, which is another reason why I've never understood how he could have killed someone in a fight, even if it was over a girl.

Anton helps me gather my clothes. I figure I can wash the wet stuff back at the flat.

'Steve said something the other night,' I say.

'Yeah?'

'Yeah. While you were asleep. I asked him how he knew you.'

Anton waves some red cotton undies at me. 'These are cute.'

'Piss off, will ya? Anyway, I asked him, and he reckons he knew you from the hostel.'

'Yep.'

'Said he used to work there.'

Anton arches one eyebrow, which is this pretty neat skill he has. He only does it occasionally, which I think gives it more impact. 'That's what he told you?'

'Yeah.'

'Well.' He smiles. 'S'pose it's true then, isn't it?'

And that's all he says on the subject. But I get the message. Actually, I get two messages. One is –

I don't really like talking about the hostel so much
and the other one is –
Steve is lying about working there.

* * *

On Johnston Street, there are lots of blokes with beards like bushrangers, which is kind of ridiculous really. Anton reckons it's pretty funny how they're all trying to be different, but look exactly the same – beards and moustaches and lots of tattoos.

Anton has a couple of tattoos himself, but they're on his back, so you never really see them. One is pretty lame – it's of a dragon breathing fire out of its mouth – and the other one is the name of his mum, Cheryl.

He told me once that Cheryl died in a car crash. When I asked what happened, he told me she was driving very fast on her own, and she hit a tree.

'Police reckon she didn't use the brakes,' he said.

So I didn't ask any more about it.

I don't have any tattoos. It's just not my thing, and they're pretty expensive. Apart from that, I don't like how they're permanent, because you might change your mind later, but you're stuck with it.

I got my nipple pierced once and it hurt like hell. I can't even remember why I did it, just a spur of the moment thing. I got a small silver ring and the lady, who was this massive dyke, said I'd have to keep it clean and make sure it didn't get infected. Anyway, I don't think she knew what she was doing, because that thing never healed in two years, and it must have got infected about a dozen times. It was pretty terrible.

Eventually, I got a different piercing place to take it out. It was such a relief. But after that, because of the scar tissue, one nipple is bigger than the other. A couple of my clients like that for some reason, and always go for the bigger one. I actually don't mind getting my nipples sucked, as long as the guy isn't too gross, and definitely not when it was infected.

Anyway, we've gone via Johnston Street because I need to go past the healthcare centre to pick up some syringes. Anton waits outside with Sunny.

I have to queue up for a bit because it's the same counter where they hand out methadone and all that. And Jenny spots me waiting.

'Hello stranger!' she calls out.

It's kind of embarrassing, and the others in the queue look back at me.

I wave. Known Jenny for a few years now, but haven't been coming here since we've been at the park. There's a place in Lygon Street that's closer, but it's not as nice as this one. The people, I mean.

When I get to the front, she gives me this big smile and pushes the brown paper bag across the counter. I like the fact that I don't have to ask. But part of me doesn't too.

'Keeping okay?' she says. I can see the way she's studying me, looking for clues.

'Yeah, just haven't been round here much.'

'Fair enough.'

She shoots a quick look at my arms.

'We've, ah, got some new programs here now. New

doctors. Some nice ones.' She slides a pamphlet across the counter, like she's done a thousand times. 'If you... you know.'

I don't want to be rude, so I take it.

twelve

It looks like Steve has gone out somewhere, which is kind of a relief. I check his room by knocking a few times, but there's no answer. I try to open it, but it's locked, which is a bit weird for a bedroom. Especially if no one is in there.

There's no lock on the handle, but about two-thirds of the way up the door there's a steel latch. It has a brass padlock looped through it.

'See this?'

Anton looks up from the couch. 'What?'

'Got a padlock.'

'So?'

'Bit weird, don't you reckon?'

He puts on the TV. 'Yeah, I s'pose. But if he's cooking in there, that might explain it.'

'True.'

I reach up and give the padlock a shake.

'Leave it,' he says.

Maybe Anton's right – maybe Steve is cooking in there. Or maybe it's locked because of Mary. When she was flipping out, maybe Steve was worried she might go into his room and trash the joint. People who flip out can think and do all sorts of crazy shit. You meet plenty of them on the street.

There's ones who think they can talk to God or something, which is pretty run of the mill, and ones who hear voices and have long conversations with themselves. You probably see those ones pretty regular. They're usually harmless, and I suppose the good thing is they're never lonely. But the bad part is the voices can sometimes tell them to do some pretty awful things.

But the ones who see things that aren't there are probably the scariest, because they can easily end up killing people. They don't even go to jail for it, but get sent to the loony bin out at Fairfield. I know a few people who've been out there, and none of them liked it very much.

Anton turns up the volume on the TV and it's a game show or some crap, but I'm not really interested in watching. I'm getting edgy and it makes it hard to concentrate on anything, even some stupid game show.

That's part of what people don't understand about being on it – when they say things like 'get your life together', or 'get a job', or stuff like that. To do those things you have to be able to concentrate, and it's really hard to concentrate when your mind is jumping, and you're feeling sick, and you know there's only one thing to make it better.

That's partly why it's hard to get straight. I say 'partly', because that's more honest. Some people will try to tell you how they're victims, and everything went wrong for them, and that kind of story. That's only partly true as well. It's mostly a combination of things, I reckon.

'Got any money left?' I say.

Anton keeps watching the show with its blue and red lights and some slick-looking guy in a suit. 'Nah. But you're gonna wear a groove if you keep that up.'

'What?'

'Pacing up and down like that.'

'What about all the stuff?'

'What stuff?'

'The stuff you'd nicked.'

He shrugs. 'Steve must've gone to pawn it.'

To be honest, at times like this, even though I really like

Anton, like a brother almost, he gets on my nerves something fierce. I don't think he gets the same withdrawals from his script stuff. Actually, I know he definitely doesn't get it as bad, because that's one of the reasons he's not on it. Reckons coming down off the gear drives him kind of insane.

I try watching TV for a bit, but that doesn't work. So I get up and have a look around the room.

There are Collingwood posters and scarves and even a gold-framed picture of one of the players, which is signed, but I can't tell you who it is, because football doesn't interest me one bit. I think Steve said it was Mary who was the fan, which makes sense because Steve doesn't seem like the sporty type. I wouldn't have a clue what Steve is into, but I reckon it would be something pretty gloomy.

There's the old timber dresser with the booze on it. There's some Southern Comfort, which is supposed to be a bourbon drink for women, but it's actually pretty disgusting. I was never into drinking that much. When I was young I was, but everyone was back then. One of my fosters used to give me Mississippi Moonshine, which was like an even cheaper and more disgusting version of Southern.

Anton thinks I've got a 'bad association' with alcohol. I've probably got a few 'bad associations', if I think about it.

'It's B!' Anton shouts at the TV. 'What an idiot!'

Still, I have a good swig, and it's as disgusting as I remember. Might at least take the edge off. I open the drawers of the dresser and there are dinner plates, cutlery, and crap like that, but there's a photo album as well. It has a horse on the front, standing in a paddock.

I open the album, and there are some pretty boring photos of the sea and mountains and things like that, like when someone goes on holiday and thinks everything looks interesting, but it actually isn't. Then there are some photos of a woman, who I'm guessing is Mary, because she's outside a football ground and is wearing the same Collingwood scarf that's hanging up over the dresser, or one just like it.

'Jesus, it's 1788!' Anton says. 'How does she not know that?'

She's pretty.

She has long, black curly hair and dark eyes and looks a bit like a Muslim, but isn't wearing the hajibi or whatever they call it. I think the photos must have been at a big game, because there are heaps of people there. There are some photos of the game itself that are pretty crap, because they were too far away from the action. I think Collingwood must have won though, because there are pictures of Mary looking happy and waving her scarf around, and then one of her and a guy with his arm around her shoulder. It looks like Steve, but a younger version – not as skinny. And it's almost like she's his girlfriend or something, even though she looks a bit older than him.

It's strange. I mean, I didn't really think Mary and Steve were in a relationship, which might sound weird, seeing how they're living together. But sometimes people shack up out of convenience. A bit like me and Anton – there's nothing romantic, it's just that life is hard on your own. Multiply that by about a hundred if you're on the street, then by another hundred if you're a girl.

'It was Richmond!' Anton yells at the TV. 'Bartlett played for Richmond! Fair dinkum.'

Steve has never called Mary his girlfriend and, as far as I can tell, doesn't seem too worried that she's been locked away for losing her marbles. I kind of assumed they were just friends who maybe used together, but I don't really know if Mary used or not. I suppose, now I think about it, I don't know very much about either of them.

I've almost forgotten about wanting a hit, but you never really completely forget about that. It's like a ringing in your ears that won't go away, but sometimes it's louder and so high-pitched that it's just unbearable. That's what it can be like. But at the moment, it's down to a low hum.

'Come have a look at this,' I say.

'What?'

'Photo album.'

'During the ads.'

And it's right then that Steve comes through the front door like some kind of cold and violent storm.

thirteen

'Where the fuck have you two been?'

I look at Anton and we both agree, without saying a word, that it isn't the best time to talk about our trip to the park.

Steve isn't really expecting an answer anyway, because he doesn't pause before launching into a long and crazy rant about his journey to the pawnbroker, and how he had to steal a shopping trolley because he couldn't carry the stuff himself, and how the cops followed him, and how it was all just a complete fucking nightmare.

I don't think it's really as much of a big deal as he's making out, but it isn't the best time to say that either.

Thing is, he doesn't yell or anything. He just kind of speaks out of the side of his mouth and clenches his fists like he's trying to hold something in, but it isn't really working. He breathes in and out really deeply, and Sunny comes right up close beside me. Like he senses something.

Because he's so caught up in his rant about the pawnshop, Steve doesn't seem to notice I'm holding the photo album behind my back. Just as well.

As it turns out, he's gotten enough from the pawnshop to score, but not as much as he was hoping for. Thing is, the pawnshop isn't a real pawnshop anyway, it's just this old Italian guy named Emilio, who everyone knows. He's in a backstreet in Fitzroy and he just sells shit out of the front room of his house. His son used to help him, but he died a few years back when he 'accidentally' fell off one of those multi-level car parks in the city. Since they put the fences on the West Gate Bridge, a lot of people accidentally fell off those.

Apparently Emilio never asks for ID or anything, which is great, but it also means he pays pretty much fuck all. He knows you have nowhere else to go if the gear is hot.

He's also sleazy as hell, which is how I know him. I've given him a hand job a few times, and every time he tries to talk me down on price. 'A real piece of work,' Anton says. Not that Cash Converters and those places would be much better. Probably just as mean, minus the hand jobs.

Anyway, after Steve calms down, he gets the gear out. Eyes me.

'You're not getting any,' he says.

'Why?'

'Not till you promise something.'

'Jesus. Okay, what?'

'That you'll go out tomorrow.'

'Out?'

'Begging.'

'Yeah,' I say, 'of course.'

If I'm honest, he could have asked me pretty much anything in that moment, holding the bag out in front of my eyes.

Begging is really no big deal.

* * *

Me and Sunny have got a new spot, which is also on Swanston Street, but out front of the library. There are two reasons I've decided to go there.

The main one is because it's under cover – the library is an old building and there's one of those enormous patio type things with huge concrete columns, like it was supposed to be in ancient Greece or something. Anton says that a lot of those old buildings were from the gold rush days, and that's why they're so completely over the top. He reckons people back then were trying to show off to England, like they'd made it big and weren't just a bunch of convicts. I don't know how he knows that, or even if it's true, but it sounds like it could be.

The other reason is because it's set a fair way back from the street. There's this big garden with lawns out front, where people sometimes eat their lunch, or smoke, or do whatever, so it isn't like I'm right on the footpath.

I know it means less people will go past, and I probably won't make as much money, but I don't like being right at people's feet. Even if it's for cash, and even if it's easy, it kind of makes me feel like crap.

It might be hard to understand, especially when I'll turn tricks with all sorts for cash, but I don't like asking for charity. If I have to work for it, it's okay. I know my clients think they're screwing me, but I reckon I'm screwing them a bit too. I'm in control, mostly.

* * *

Me and Sunny have been here for a while and it's going pretty well. It's a different crowd, but still a real mix. Most of them are students probably, but it's hard to tell. There are a lot of Asians. Heaps. But not many of them have given me anything.

To be fair, I think some are scared of Sunny, which is probably understandable. I think they have dogs in China or wherever, but probably not big dogs like him. Some people might make a joke about Asians and dogs, but not me. I like Asians, especially Vietnamese, because they're usually the most friendly. Except for Paul, but not liking him has got nothing to do with him being Asian.

I had a regular client once named Tommy, who was just this young guy whose real name was Tuan, but he took ages to tell me that. He was clean and gentle and just a nice kid who was screwing up majorly at uni, but couldn't tell his parents. It's funny what people will tell you about sometimes. Anton says being a hooker is a bit like being a hairdresser – people tell you their secrets.

Tommy also told me about chasing the dragon, which I thought I knew about, but he had a whole different explanation. He said the dragon was like this curse on the Vietnamese that means bad shit happens to them all the time, like they're being chased by this dragon. Smoking heroin was meant to chase the dragon back.

Even though I liked that story, it seemed to me that chasing the dragon would definitely make things worse. But I'm not anyone to be giving lectures.

I'd always understood it different, maybe because I never smoked it. I thought the dragon was the first hit you ever had. It was that warm, weightless feeling you never saw coming, when everything suddenly made sense, and you thought nothing would ever worry you again. That was the dragon. And we're all chasing it, even if we know, deep down, we'll never find it again.

I'm getting off track a bit, but it's important to explain things sometimes, because otherwise people might think you're a bit shallow, you know? Like, I've got a story too. I've got a history and there are things that happened. Just because I don't talk about those things much, doesn't mean they aren't real – I just don't like to make excuses. There's no point. A lot of people on the street and a lot of people everywhere make excuses. I don't want to be like that.

But there's a difference between reasons and excuses. I'm not sure I can explain exactly what it is, but there's definitely a difference.

* * *

It's started raining pretty heavy, so I'm glad for being under cover. Then one of the library people, a woman who walks like she's pretty important, comes out. Black skirt and shiny heels. Hard eyes and red lipstick.

'You can't stay here.'

'Why?'

Shakes her head. 'Sorry, you'll just have to move on.'

I look out to where the rain is getting heavier, hoping she might change her mind. She turns and heads back inside without another word.

I decide she can stick it. I mean, honestly, what difference does it make to her if I'm out the front or not? People are still coming to the library, and I'm not hassling anyone, or being abusive.

Look, I know it's probably not ideal to have a beggar at your front door. Like, it's not the best look I suppose, if tourists or whatever are coming. But that isn't my problem.

* * *

Dirty Doug arrives maybe half an hour later. It's a bit of an overreaction by the library witch.

'What a surprise.'

'What?'

'Knew it'd be you two.'

He gives Sunny a pat. Sunny gives him eyes like he remembers.

'How'd you know?'

He puts on his best toneless copper voice. 'Female in vicinity of State Library begging alms. Large, threatening canine.'

I laugh.

'Change of scene?' He looks out to the rain. 'Fair enough too.'

'Where's your partner?'

'Off sick.'

'You two... you know?'

'Jealous?'

'Ha!'

'So, you done here then, or what?'

I pick up my cash. 'Think so.'

'Can guess where that's going.'

I hold up the sign. 'Bus ticket to Albury.'

He sighs. 'Thought more about rehab?'

I nod. 'Yep, gonna go tomorrow. I promise. Then back to school for my VCE.'

'How's Anton?'

I loop the rope around Sunny's neck. 'Okay.'

'And the other bloke?'

'Who?'

'Don't play smart. Petrovic. I saw you walking with him the other night.'

Petrovic. Steve Petrovic. It suits him somehow.

'That who you're staying with?'

'You stalking me?'

'He's got a long history.'

I shrug. 'What else is new?'

But I can tell Dirty Doug isn't joking around, because he gets his proper copper face on, which he hardly ever does.

'Listen, he's pretty volatile.'

'What do you mean?'

He hesitates, rubs his chin like he's weighing something up. Looks out to the street. 'I... I can't say much more. Privacy and all that, you know. Have to be careful these days.'

Sunny pulls at the rope, like he's keen to get moving.

'Only staying while his girlfriend is in psych. Short-term thing.'

Petrovic. Steve Petrovic.

The rain starts to ease. Dirty Doug eyes me. Holds out his hand.

'Just be careful, yeah?'

There's a ten-dollar note folded between his fingers.

I smile. 'Thanks. Yep, no need to worry.'

fourteen

On the way back to the flat, I take a shortcut through the Carlton Gardens. They're the gardens where the Exhibition Building is, so a lot of people call it the Exhibition Gardens, but that isn't right.

I haven't been in the Exhibition Building before, but it's supposed to be pretty nice. They have car shows and bridal expos and stuff like that, but you have to pay to get in. The car shows might be all right, if you're into that type of thing, but the bridal shows are just completely ridiculous. I mean, why would you go pay to look at a wedding dress? Some people are crazy.

Anyway, I always like walking through the gardens because they have beautiful old trees and a big water fountain that looks like it should be in Europe, or somewhere. Me and Anton once talked about moving from Princes Park to the Carlton Gardens, mainly because it was much nicer, and because it was closer to the city. But in the end, Anton decided we shouldn't for a couple of reasons.

First, he reckoned there wasn't as many places under cover, so it would be pretty rough in winter. Second, he'd heard you could get into more trouble around there, mainly because of the mentally ill people who get let out of St Vincent's. Plus, a lot of people walk through on their way to work in the mornings, so it'd be hard to get any privacy.

So there were actually three reasons, but the first two were the main ones.

It's almost dark and it's started to rain again, but not as heavy this time. Sunny is always happy to go through the gardens because he gets to sniff and piss on pretty much everything. I untie his rope and let him loose and he's totally loving it. The gardens are pretty well lit, which is good for safety, but would probably be terrible for sleeping. Still, some people do sleep there. And when I hear Sunny growling, which he hardly ever does, I realise he's run into someone.

* * *

I know Danny from the Salvos in the city, but also from Princes Park because he stayed there once for a couple of weeks. He's all right, but has some sort of brain injury or something.

He's a bit slow, but probably has a few other things going on as well. Psychological things. Paranoia, I reckon, because he used to always think the police were looking for him, even though he couldn't explain why, or if he'd done anything. I don't think he ever did drugs or drank or anything like that. He just had some bad luck, I suppose.

He's wearing his thick lumberjack coat, which he always has on, even when it's hot. Anton reckons that's one way to tell if people are crazy – if they dress completely inappropriate for the weather. He's got his stuff set up around a park bench, which you might think is a good choice, but it's not really. Park benches are generally out in the weather, and not the best place to leave your stuff, because people are more likely to nick it. And council workers are more likely to dump it in the rubbish, because normal people want to sit there.

That's the thing – when you're on the street, it's important not to be too conspicuous, to make yourself disappear a bit. Because if you get in the way of what normal people are doing, that's when you get into trouble.

But if you're just in the background, an inconvenience, or a bit of an eyesore, it's not so bad. People can live with that. Mostly.

Sunny starts barking at Danny. And I realise he's barking because Danny has a dog – a big dog.

'Hey,' I say.

'Hey.'

Don't think he remembers me, eyes are glassy.

'What's the dog's name?'

'Robert.'

'Nice name,' I say, even if I don't think so.

'Yep.'

'Friendly?'

Danny gives Robert a pat. 'Sometimes. Not really.'

Robert is enormous, and doesn't look like he has much patience. I think he might be one of those breeds that's banned. I tie the rope around Sunny and get him to shush.

'How have you been?' I say.

'Okay.'

'What are you doing here?'

'What do ya mean?'

'Weren't you going to a hostel?'

'Yeah.'

'What happened?'

'Had to leave.'

'Why?'

He thinks about this for a bit. 'Because of Robert.'

The conversation is only going to go so far.

'Got any food?' I say.

'Nah.'

'And you're sleeping here?'

'Yeah.'

It's probably not my place to be doing it, but I tell Danny about the flat. I ask if he might want to come crash there for the night.

'Maybe.'

'C'mon.'

'Nah.'

'Why?'

'Just... nah.'

It probably isn't the smartest idea anyway, so it's just as well. Anton doesn't mind him. Actually, Anton is probably nicer to him than anyone. He really looked after him when he was at the park. Showed him the ropes, like a big brother.

But I don't know how Steve would react.

Steve Petrovic.

'You got money?'

'Bit.'

'How much?'

He reaches into his coat pocket and pulls out a few coins. All silver.

* * *

Steve is less than impressed.

'How come there's not as much?'

'As what?'

'As last time.'

'What do you mean?'

Eyes harden. 'Don't be a smartarse.'

He shows Anton, who shrugs, but shoots me this quick look like *don't make things worse.* I can tell Steve makes him nervous.

'It was raining,' I say. 'So there was less people. Most of them just rush past, you know? Get out of the weather.'

He frowns. It's like he believes what I'm saying, but doesn't really want to. You know how some people almost like getting angry? Like part of them enjoys it? That's how it is with him, I think.

It feels like there's always something bubbling under the surface with Steve, waiting to burst out. That's the impression I get. Can't imagine ever feeling completely relaxed around him, unless we're all high. When we're high, he's fine. Fun, almost.

I'm not sure how much I gave Danny, but it was maybe half of what I'd made, including what Dirty Doug gave me. And I told him not to lose it, and to make sure he went to the Salvos so they could sort him out. I don't know if he will, though. He listened to me, but I'm not sure how much sinks in.

Like I was saying before, most people on the street are there for a mixture of reasons. There's hardly ever just one thing, you know? Like, there's things that happened when they were kids, which is bad luck, and maybe then some bad decisions, and drugs, and whatever. Once drugs and booze get into it, it's pretty hard to know exactly what caused people to end up where they are. A lot of the time, they don't even remember themselves. Anton says that social workers call it 'complex problems', or something like that.

To be fair, some people are just stupid too, and it isn't about bad luck. Some people have things pretty good, but still manage to completely fuck it up for themselves. But I suppose there's reasons for that as well.

But Danny is different. It's pretty much all down to bad luck, not bad decisions. So people like Danny need help, you know? You can't just turn your back.

But there's no way I can explain any of this to Steve. I'll tell Anton later, but definitely not Steve.

And I might tell Anton about what Dirty Doug said too.

fifteen

Doing burgs at night probably isn't the smartest thing, because most people are home. Your only hope is if people are out somewhere, or on holiday, or maybe just asleep. It's all pretty high risk.

I'm worried about Anton. If he gets caught, he'll be going back inside for sure. But it seems like Steve knows what he's doing. He has a bit of confidence about him, if that makes sense. Like, if he says he's gonna do something, he'll probably do it.

Anton's different. More unsure of himself, I suppose. I guess it might just be the way he was born, but I reckon you can become like that too.

I don't really like the idea of robbing people much. I suppose my main problem is it's so random. If you were robbing someone who was a real prick, and you knew that for sure, that would be different. But how could you know? You could be robbing someone who's sick, or really struggling, or maybe they've just managed to buy a few things after saving for years. You could never really be sure about any of it, which is why I don't like it.

But if I'm really honest – and I'm not proud to admit it – I'm pretty happy if they're gonna be able to score more gear. So it's not like I can take the high moral ground, I suppose. I guess that's what being on it does to you – you can pretty much tolerate anything, as long as it means you'll get the next hit. Maybe not anything, but most things.

Anton once told me this story about Paul, that Vietnamese dealer, but I've never known if it was true. He said Paul and his brother went back to Vietnam a few years ago, and they tried to smuggle some gear to Melbourne. Paul put the smack inside ten separate condoms, which he tied up into little balloons. He made his brother swallow them down, which would have been awful, but Anton reckons it's one of the best ways to do it.

Somehow, they got through customs and everything without a hitch. So it had all gone perfectly to plan. But then, on their way back to Paul's flat, his brother started to get sick. Really sick.

Anton says Paul didn't want to take him to hospital or anything, 'For obvious reasons,' so they went to his brother's place instead and waited to see what happened.

And what happened was his eyes rolled back in his head and his mouth started foaming. He passed out. Not long after, he stopped breathing. Apparently, some of the condoms had split open inside him. I said to Anton that maybe Paul had bought cheap ones, and he reckoned that could be true.

Either way, Paul mustn't have been very upset about it. Or maybe him and his brother didn't get along very well. Because Anton reckons Paul barely waited a minute after his brother had stopped breathing before he gutted him like a rabbit. 'Sliced him open with a kitchen knife, then scooped the condoms out.'

So that's the other reason I don't like buying off Paul so much. Probably the main reason. Like I said, I don't know for sure if it's true, but there's nothing about Paul that makes you think it isn't.

* * *

They've been gone for ages.

A distraction. That's what I need.

There's a little bit of leftover gear on the table. And it's pretty tempting just to have a taste – Steve might not even notice.

He might realise, though. He seems the type to notice something like that. And I don't know how he might react.

Volatile.

That's what Dirty Doug said.

Most users are pretty observant about how much gear is left. It's one of the few things we pay very close attention to. If anything, it's probably something we're better at than normal people. We can notice if even a tiny amount is gone. Like our special skill, I suppose.

So I'll leave it.

For now.

Actually, I'll put it up inside the kitchen cupboard, just so I'll need to get a chair or something if I change my mind, so it won't be right there in front of me like that.

* * *

God, there is such crap on TV. It seems like all the channels are the same with American crime or singing and dancing talent shows with judges who are plastic and just horrible.

I put on Channel Two and it's this show with a panel and people in the audience asking dumb questions, and it's probably the most boring thing I've ever seen in my life. It's like they think they can solve the world's problems by sitting around and talking crap.

I suppose that's one thing about being on the street – you don't watch much TV. I used to watch a bit when I was a kid, but I mostly like movies. Like I said, me and Anton snuck into the Nova sometimes, but not very much since I got Sunny.

I'm not into the big Hollywood blockbusters, so Anton reckons I'm a snob, but they seem all the same to me and really overrated. Anyway, he's probably more of a snob, because he's mostly into the arty ones too.

Probably one of his favourites is called *Dogville,* and it's about a woman who is on the run, and she goes to this little town and tries to fit in. But she's got this secret, and the people in town aren't really what they seem, and you should see it if you ever get the chance. It's got Nicole Kidman in it, but don't let that put you off.

Maybe I should just have a small taste. I don't need to shoot up, I could snort a little bit and that might take the edge off. It's not the most efficient way, but it would do the trick, and I could make sure it looked like I hadn't taken any. Just spread it around in the bag a bit.

I put the chair against the cupboard and I climb up.

No.

Need to wait until they get back. It won't be too long, and I have to be patient. Definitely.

I've got the whole flat to myself and there's the TV and stuff I can look at. Or maybe I can make something to eat. Or maybe I should take Sunny for a walk. Just something to take my mind off.

It's all getting more intense. I mean, when we were in the park I was scoring maybe every couple of days, sometimes just twice a week – like, I had things more under control, I think.

I'm using more since we've been in the flat. It's funny how quick it happens and without you really noticing. Anton said once that it's like walking out into the sea, and you think everything's fine and the water's warm, but when you turn back you're suddenly miles from shore.

I've never been much of a swimmer, but I get what he means. Like, being caught in a current or something. A rip.

I look in the fridge and there's almost nothing there, which is pretty disappointing. There's an old dried-up corncob, and I wonder if I boil that up whether it might come back to life a bit, and I could put butter on it maybe, or margarine.

I find a pot and put it on the stovetop. The stove is old and pretty filthy, like maybe cleaning isn't one of Steve and Mary's things. It takes forever to heat up, so I stand there watching and waiting for the coil to go red. I put my hand above it and it's a little bit warm, so it's definitely working, but just gonna take ages.

While I'm waiting, I have a look around Mary's room. It's also my room, sort of, so I'm probably allowed to look through the drawers and see what's there. It's not like I'm snooping through her stuff or anything. And no one will know either way.

Underwear, socks, t-shirts – nothing that special, which probably shouldn't be a surprise. There's a cupboard too with some clothes hanging up, and shoes down the bottom. There's a really fancy dress in there, almost like a bridesmaid's thing, all wrapped in plastic. And it makes me think of a formal one of my fosters made me go to once.

My foster brother took me, and he made me touch it for the first time that night, even though I told him I didn't really want to. He said it would be good practice, because if I wanted to stay with them, I'd have to be doing it regular.

I don't like thinking about that so much.

I go to the bathroom and look at myself in the mirror. I'm really beautiful with the dress on, if I do say so myself. I think if my foster brother could see me he'd be pretty shocked, and if he asked me to do it now I'd definitely say no.

I *am* beautiful, even if the dress is a bit tight. I find some lipstick which must be Mary's, so I try that on, and there's some makeup and hairspray, and even a hairbrush, and I wonder why Mary hasn't taken any of these things with her to the psych hospital. And I wonder if that's where she really is.

Just be careful.

That's what Dirty Doug said.

He's got a long history.

* * *

'What gave you the fucking right?'

Steve's face is red. Furious. But his words just float above me.

'Calm down,' Anton says, 'these things happen.'

They must be surprised to see me wearing the dress and makeup.

They're probably more surprised about the smell, because I'd forgotten the pot on the stove and the handle has melted and the corn has shrivelled up into something black and horrible.

Steve knew straight away something was up, because he didn't even bother with the stove. To be honest, it's lucky they came home when they did, or I probably would have burnt the place down.

'You're gonna pay for it,' Steve says. 'One way or another.'

It might have been a mistake to use all of it, because Steve probably isn't the sort of person who'll let something like that slide. I don't really know what kind of person he is, if I'm honest, but I don't think he's the type who just forgets about things like that.

sixteen

I can't be sure he hasn't been doing it in secret, but I don't think so. Still, couldn't say for certain.

Anton has started injecting. At least, it's the first time I've seen him do it. First time ever, actually.

You can never be sure with anyone about anything, but especially when you're using. People are pretty good at hiding things when they want to. And when you're using, you don't tend to notice as much. It isn't a good combination.

Once Steve has a hit, things calm down. We don't listen to music, because the TV is on and I think everyone is a bit sleepy, and it's kind of nice to sit there quiet and watch an old black-and-white movie. This one's called *The Devil and Daniel Webster* and I've never seen it before, but it's about a farmer who sells his soul.

When it's over, Steve turns to me.

'Why are you wearing that dress?'

I shrug.

'Never seen you in a dress,' he says.

'Me either,' Anton says. His eyes are almost closed. It's hit him really hard.

'Mary's,' I say.

'Probably right,' Steve says, like he's never seen it before. I figure it's a bit strange if Mary was his girlfriend, but I suppose men don't notice things like that sometimes. Still, I decide to ask him straight up.

'Is Mary your girlfriend?'

He just keeps looking at the TV like he hasn't heard. The credits are rolling, but they don't last long. Then he looks at me and says, 'Something like that,' which is pretty much the end of the conversation.

He has this way of showing he doesn't want to talk about things by looking at you so sharply, and so quickly, that you're not sure if he did it. But he looks, just for a split second, like he wants to cut your throat. He does it so quick that you almost think you've imagined it.

'How come she didn't take her stuff?' I say.

'What?'

'Her toiletries and that. They're all still here.'

That look again.

'How should I know?'

Anton gets the nods something terrible. I think he isn't used to anything so strong, so I decide I'll have to stay awake to keep an eye on him. When people die of an overdose, it's really quiet and subtle, so most times the people around them don't even notice until the next day. Or the day after that. It isn't like in the movies.

'Anton,' I say. 'Where did you go tonight?'

I have to say his name a few times before he opens his eyes a little. He smiles this sleepy grin and points at Steve.

Steve says, 'Does it matter?'

Anton closes his eyes again.

'Just trying to keep him awake.'

Steve dismisses me with a wave. 'He'll be right.'

'Should be more careful,' I say. 'He'll end up back in jail.'

'He won't,' Steve says. 'We won't.'

'How can you be sure?'

The look. Again.

'If you got more money begging, wouldn't be a problem.'

'You could try something else,' I say.

'Like what?'

'Dunno. Window washing, maybe.'

He gets this smirk. 'You've got to be fucking joking.'

It's like the whole idea is completely beneath him. Like he's royalty or something.

I think that might be the thing – he thinks he's better than everyone. Superior. Like everyone else is stupid. Like life is just a game, and only he knows the rules. It annoys me.

'Why don't you go sell *The Big Issue* then, or something?'

He laughs like it's this massive joke.

'Do I look retarded?'

I tell Anton to wake up. Loudly. His eyelids flicker.

'Anton,' I say. 'Do you want a glass of water?'

Coughs, eyes still closed. 'Nah.'

'Just try to stay awake. Okay?'

Steve laughs quietly to himself, stifles it, but I hear.

Sunny puts his head on my lap, looks up at me like he might be hungry. I can hardly move. Everything is so heavy. Arms and legs like lead.

Steve starts talking about *The Big Issue,* and then he starts up about capitalism, then communism, and Anton is fast asleep now. I watch him closely, make sure he keeps breathing.

Chest up and down.

In and out.

So slowly.

I wish he wasn't sleeping. I wish he'd stay awake. And that I could stay awake too. But you can only listen to someone like Steve bang on like that for so long.

seventeen

When I wake, it takes me a while to realise where I am. My head is like rubber.

Anton isn't around. Neither is Steve. His door is locked up.

The smell is really strong now. In everything – its sourness makes me queasy. A bitter taste on my tongue.

I'm usually the first up out of me and Anton, but this gear has really knocked me around. Must be about two in the afternoon, I think, and I check the fridge. Someone already got bread – it's white bread, and I eat a couple of slices just standing there in the kitchen. Thick saliva, hard to swallow. Sunny is on the couch where Anton had been sleeping. He comes over. I give him a slice of bread, which he half chokes on. Then I give him another.

They must have gone to do another burg or something. Last night they'd come back so quick with the gear, so I figure whatever they'd stolen, they must have traded directly.

I'm not really sure what to do. I could go begging again, but I don't really feel like it. It makes for a pretty long day. In all honesty, if I turned a couple of tricks I could make the same cash easy enough, but I'm not in the mood for that either.

If they manage to get some cash, they'll probably have more gear and maybe I don't even need to bother with going out anywhere, or doing anything. Maybe I might just get looked after from now on. I doubt it. Steve doesn't seem the type who likes freeloaders.

I wonder if he could have gone to see Mary, and maybe Anton has gone too. But it doesn't make much sense that Anton would go, especially without telling me.

I think again of Mary's toiletries and her stuff in the bathroom. I suppose she might have been taken away all of a sudden, with a van and people in white coats, but I think that only happens in the movies. And even if she did go like that, I reckon she would have got Steve to bring her things.

I mean, I'm no detective, but it seems a bit strange that all her stuff is still here, and all pristine. A few things seem strange, now I think about it.

And the smell. The smell is definitely worse.

Steve's room.

I go to his door. The smell seems stronger there, but it's hard to be sure. It's everywhere.

If he's cooking meth, and the cops come, we all go down in one way or another. Anton for sure. Bottom line – if Steve is cooking, we've got to get out of here.

Why does he have a different bedroom if him and Mary are together? Never thought to ask. I mean, only old people sleep in different bedrooms, I think.

I look at the latch. The padlock is brass and I suppose Steve must keep the key with him. The screws are the flathead type with slots, not the star ones. I don't know what you call them, but I reckon I might be able to unscrew them with a knife or something. Might not need a screwdriver. Just to have a quick look while they're out. See what he's up to in there.

Whack whack.

Steel clang – aluminium.

Whack whack.

Two sharp knocks at the door.

I freeze. Wait a few seconds. Hold my breath.

Whack whack whack.

Again. Harder this time.

Sunny barks. *Shhh.*

Whack whack.

They're not giving up. I go to the door. Open it slowly.

An old lady, maybe in her sixties or seventies. Greek or Italian. Can never tell. She's very small and squints at me through scratched, thick-lensed glasses that look about a hundred years old.

'Hello,' she says. 'Maria?'

'Maria?'

'I look for Maria.'

Mary.

'Ah, she's not here.'

'Who are you?'

'I live here,' I say.

'You live?'

'Yeah. I mean, I'm staying here.'

She frowns. 'I'm next door. Maria? She your friend?'

'I suppose. Um, sort of.'

'Where she?'

'Gone away... for a bit, I think.'

Pauses.

'The man?' She tries to look past me, inside.

'Who?'

'Tall man, skinny. He there?'

Steve. Steve Petrovic.

'Not now, no.'

'He come, you know? Then I no see.'

'No see?'

'No see Maria anymore.'

Sunny sits at my feet. I'm not sure what to say.

'She... I think she went to stay with family.'

The lady sniffs, lips curl. 'What is that?'

'What?'

Sniffs again. 'That... that smell?'

Sunny lets out a long sigh. Lies down.

'I... I better go.'

She nods, but doesn't answer.

I don't want to lie about it, but I don't know if I should tell her about the psych hospital. I mean, that's pretty private. You wouldn't really want your neighbours knowing, I wouldn't think. Besides, I can't be completely sure if it's true.

He come. Then I no see.

The door. The lock. The screws.

I'm sure I can get it done quickly. Before they get back.

It might be nothing – no meth or anything. The lock could just be a habit, or maybe something he's been doing for years. That happens sometimes. Like, when kids have got brothers who go through their stuff, they get a lock on the door, and then they get used to having that. So even when they're older, and their brothers aren't around, they still do it.

But it's hard to imagine Steve doing anything just out of habit. It's even harder to imagine him being a kid.

Maybe something died under the house. A rat or something. Or in the walls. Could be that.

I get a knife from the kitchen.

A steak knife, but the tip is too pointy. I get a regular knife and start in on one of the screws, but it's really hard going. I try another one and get it to turn a bit, then I damage the slot and can't get it to move again. It's pretty frustrating, and just makes me want to get inside there even more.

There are six screws in all, and I figure that if I can get the other four, then maybe the whole thing will come loose. The first two take ages, but I'm more patient and go more slowly this time, so I don't damage them. It takes a while, and my wrist is really sore, but I eventually get them out.

Sunny starts whining, like he needs to go out for a piss or something. But he's pissed inside plenty of times already, and I'm on a bit of a roll and have nearly got the third one out, so I don't want to stop while I've got some rhythm.

'Shhh,' I say.

I stop to give him a pat, quieten him down.

And then, behind me, I hear the front door swing wide open.

eighteen

Can't open my eyes. Not right away. Can open the right one a bit, but the left one is stuck together, almost like it's glued shut.

A deep throbbing around my nose. Go to touch it.

'Shhh.'

Someone takes my hand.

Can feel him sitting on the edge of the bed beside me. His warmth.

Anton.

'Drink?'

He places his hand behind my back and helps me sit up, brings the glass to my lips. It tastes a bit funny, but the water is cool and fresh in my mouth.

My whole head begins to pulse, like it has its own heart-beat. Lie back down.

'Try to sleep,' he says.

* * *

Hours later. Don't know how many.

I wake, and can open my right eye a little more this time.

I'm in Mary's room – my room – and it's light outside. My nose is still throbbing, but not quite as bad. Deeper.

Something pretty terrible has happened. And it's happened

to me. It's hard to breathe through my nose – I wonder if it's broken and maybe that's why my eye is shut too.

I hope that's all that happened.

Can't remember, not exactly, but I know it wasn't Anton. Couldn't be. It was almost definitely Steve who did this to me.

It probably wasn't the smartest thing – to try to open that door, I mean. I'm not sure what I was thinking. I know what I was looking for, but the timing was all wrong – just didn't expect them to come back so soon.

I have a feel of my nose. The skin and flesh is numb, the pain somewhere underneath. It feels enormous under my fingertips. Lumpy. Swollen. A crisp scab of dried blood between my eyes. I sit up a little – Christ, my head hurts.

Decide to get up.

Go to Mary's dresser.

Look in the mirror.

* * *

Anton hears me and comes in quick, even though I'm trying hard to be quiet.

'Shhh,' he says.

I sob, my throat raw.

'That cunt,' I say.

'It's not as bad as you think.'

'What? Don't you see this?'

He glances at the mirror, looks away. Can't meet my eyes.

'Once the swelling goes down, you'll be pretty much—'

'Are you serious?'

He takes my hand, leads me back to the bed, sits beside me.

'You'll get pretty much back to normal. Promise. Then you can get it straightened at the Eye and Ear Hospital. I had it done once. Doesn't even hurt.' He wiggles his nose between his fingers. 'All cartilage in there.'

He wipes the tears from my cheeks.

'Why'd he do it?' I say.

Shakes his head.

'Dunno. But he shouldn't have.'

'He's a fucking psycho.'

Anton nods. 'So, do you wanna?'

'What?' I say.

'You know. Might help.'

* * *

We share the same needle, which is something I always try to avoid. But seeing it's Anton, I'm guessing it's probably okay. Jenny at the healthcare centre would be furious.

'Should rest for a few days.'

'Yep.'

'Steve reckons you can't go out like that.'

'Begging?'

'Yeah.'

'He's worried?'

'About what?'

Anton's eyes have already gone sleepy. He squints. Lips curl into dream.

'Dunno. That I'll go to the cops?'

He doesn't answer.

Thing is, and Anton knows it, I don't really have any intention. It'll just complicate things, and they'll do nothing.

Shit versus shit – that's what they say.

Dirty Doug might be different. If I tell Dirty Doug, he'll do something.

But I don't want him to see me like this. Don't want him to think I'm going backwards. Maybe once my face is better, but not now.

* * *

About to go again. Before we do, I ask him.

'We're getting out of here, right?'

Doesn't answer. Looks for a good vein in his arm. There aren't many.

'Anton? We're gonna leave, right?'

Eyes meet mine. 'Yeah, soon.'

'When?'

'When we start to get back on top of things, you know? Once you can go out again.'

'What about Steve,' I say. 'He's... he's crazy. And Dirty Doug said—'

I watch as he sinks the needle into his wrist, which is honestly one of the most painful spots, but usually good for veins. He doesn't flinch.

'Doug?' Eyes widen. 'When did you see him?'

'He said to be careful, you know? About Steve.'

He pushes the plunger all the way down and lets out a long breath. He takes the needle out, puts his thumb over the vein.

'Hear what I said?'

'Yeah.' Doesn't look me in the eyes.

'Where is he?'

'Dunno.'

'Sunny?'

'Took him.'

My face goes hot.

'What?'

'Don't worry.'

Anton gets me a clean syringe.

'You sure? I don't trust him. Even with Sunny, he could—'

'He'll be right.'

I take the syringe out of its wrapper.

'But we're gonna go though?' I say. 'Even just back to the park.'

Thing is, I can tell he's getting used to staying here. More than that, he's used to being back on the gear again. And when that's got hold of you, it's hard to make plans. And even harder to do anything about them.

'What about saving some cash first?' he says. 'For the flat and all that. For the bond so–'

'The flat? The bond? Fucking hell, Anton, get real. Look at me... look at what he did.'

His cheeks flush.

'I'm sorry, you know. It's not like... I mean, I didn't know that was gonna happen.'

'Right.'

'And it's not like I didn't stick up for you.'

I glare. He avoids my gaze.

'He wanted to chuck you out. After, I mean.'

I don't answer. I look for the good vein on the inside of my thigh. It isn't quite as good anymore.

'Yeah,' he says. 'But I stopped him.'

I don't know if this is true or not, or if Anton is just trying to make himself look better.

'Just a few more weeks,' he says.

'Really?'

'Yeah. Just a couple more burgs. I'll keep some of the cash, then we'll go.'

'Three weeks?'

'Yep.'

'How about two?'

He smiles. 'Fair enough, two then.'

I pull what's left into the syringe.

'Why'd you do it though?' he says.

'What?'

'The door?'

'That smell,' I say. 'Doesn't it make you wonder? And the lock?'

Anton lies back on the bed and closes his eyes. 'None of my business, I s'pose.'

And that's pretty much the last thing he says about it. And I get the feeling this time that it isn't about his principles, or anything like that.

I get the feeling Anton might be a bit scared of Steve. And it's probably fair enough.

Just two more weeks, though. Definitely.

nineteen

I decide, for a few days at least, not to look in the mirror. It's easier said than done – it's not something you normally think about, but you see yourself in mirrors a lot. Especially when you brush your teeth, and stuff like that.

It doesn't look good. I know the cut will heal and the swelling will go down and I won't have black eyes forever, but my nose is in pretty bad shape.

It's moved about half a centimetre to the left. I don't think that can be fixed at the Eye and Ear Hospital, or anywhere else. My right cheek is huge, like a purple mango, and I wonder if he broke my cheekbone. It still hurts like hell, but at least I can move my jaw. Might be fractured.

Luckily, I've still got my teeth, so I'm guessing he just hit me twice – left then right – and that's all I needed.

Two weeks.

That's what Anton said.

I'll make sure he sticks to it. And if he doesn't want to leave, I'm going without him. I don't want to be on my own, but I can't stay with Steve.

Two weeks – that's it.

I'm a bit worried if some of the damage to my face might be permanent. Look, I'm probably no glamour model at the best of times, pretty average I suppose, but not too bad. So I wonder what it will mean for my work.

If I'm permanently like this, then blokes won't want to pay much. Or I'll end up only with the horrible ones – the ones into strange stuff. Some of them treat girls like animals. They tend to go for the rougher-looking ones, because I suppose they figure they're more likely to take it and not complain. Because they need the money. We all need the money.

Not that there's anyone to complain to, anyway. I've heard there's a website or something, but what's the point?

It's probably better if I don't tell you all the things some of them want, because you'd be pretty grossed out. A lot of pedo role-play stuff. And the girls who look really young always make the most. Anton reckons it's probably better those guys are doing it with hookers, rather than with their daughters or nieces or whatever. But how do you know they're not doing both?

As you can imagine, those ones would rather a girl on the street than one in a brothel – they can get away with more that way. Most brothels are a bit stricter, except some of the Asian joints who have got young girls there basically like slaves. I've heard some real horror stories.

But honestly, most of my blokes are pretty vanilla. And I want to keep it that way.

* * *

Third day in the bedroom – there's a knock at the door. And I know it can't be Anton. He never knocks.

Steve opens it before I have a chance to answer. My heart pumps hard and fast and I can't make it slow. He stands in the doorway for a bit, looking at me, like he's surveying the damage.

Smiles, but I can tell he's forcing it.

'How you going?' he says.

'Okay.'

Looks a bit more sheepish than normal, eyes down.

'Need anything?'

'Nah.'

He stays in the doorway, holding the handle like he doesn't really want to come in, but knows he shouldn't just walk off. I feel a rush of heat rising in my chest. It's anger, but something else too.

'Don't cry,' he says. Shakes his head, 'Jesus.'

I wipe my cheeks, my eyes.

'I'm fine.'

He goes quiet. And there's something about him which reminds me of a little kid. He's like a teenager who's doing something they know they're supposed to, but don't really want to. It sounds strange to say it, but – for just a second – I almost feel sorry for him.

'I'm ah...'

'Yeah?'

'I'm... I'm really sorry. About what happened, I mean.'

I nod.

'But, you know.'

He looks down at his feet. It's all so horrible and awkward.

'I probably shouldn't have...' I say, 'the door, I mean.'

He nods.

'Still,' he says, 'probably overdid it.'

'Yep. Probably.'

'Anton's pretty pissed at me too.'

I'm glad to hear that, but I don't show it.

He looks up at me again. Flinches.

'That bad?'

'It'll get better.' He swings the door slowly back and forth, like he's checking its hinges. 'Walked Sunny for you.'

'Thanks.'

And that's the closest I get to an apology.

To be fair, he did say sorry, and I wasn't really expecting that. Besides, I wasn't that interested in hearing him be all remorseful. I've always felt like apologies are mostly useless, because I've heard them plenty of times, and they don't really mean anything. People usually just keep doing exactly the same things anyway.

Anton reckons past behaviour is usually the best predictor of future behaviour. He's said it more than once. And he's probably right about that.

Still, Steve must have felt a bit bad. He doesn't seem like the sort who 'does' apologies, if you know what I mean. Or maybe he's worried about me going to the cops.

Probably that, I reckon. More likely.

* * *

Anton gave me some of his Endone, and that's been a big help to get me through the day. Until we shoot up, anyway.

They're still going out and doing burgs, but I've stopped worrying so much about Anton. I figure they've had a bit of practice now and probably know what they're doing.

Anton tells me how late morning is usually the best, because people have gone to work and there's plenty of time till school finishes, and no one will have come home for lunch, which apparently some people do.

Then he explained the whole process, and he was almost like a kid who was telling his mum about something good he learned about at school. He reckoned Steve had taught him pretty much everything he knew, and it was going to be a really handy skill from now on.

Basically, they pick a house which looks like a family joint. If there are kids (and therefore, most likely, a mum), there'd usually be jewellery. 'Not always,' Anton said, 'but a lot of the time.' They also try to pick places with high fences or trees out front, so it's hard to see them from the street.

Anton knocks on the door to see if anyone's home. If someone answers, he says, 'Is Matty around?' then 'realises' he has the wrong address. All of which is bullshit, of course.

But if no one is home, he looks for a spare key first. He reckons people put them 'in all sorts of dumb places', and one time the front door was actually just open. Once he's in,

Steve goes and tries to get a taxi to wait out front. That's their getaway vehicle, if he can get one.

Anton goes for the main bedroom first, because that's usually where watches and jewellery and sometimes even cash are kept, then the kitchen and lounge for any electronics. He said student houses are great too, because they have heaps of electronics and things like that, but they're also higher risk because students have irregular hours and can come home anytime. 'The last thing we want is a confrontation,' he said.

But, like I say, Anton has principles – these rules for how he lives. He usually wouldn't steal from anyone, so you might wonder why he's so excited about doing these burgs.

But he isn't really excited – that's the thing. He sounds like he is, but if you really know him, you can tell it isn't really him talking. There's something dull in his eyes – a bit empty, almost like he's in some kind of trance.

And it reminds me of what he said before, about being in the sea. I know what he means now, because I can see it in his eyes. That distance. He's adrift – we both are – pulled further and further out. My hand holding his, only just hanging on.

We're past the breakers now, in open water, and miles from shore. I can't see it, but know it must be there, somewhere beyond the horizon.

Two more weeks.

That's what he said.

twenty

Since I got out of bed, I've been watching a lot of TV. But not really watching, you know? Like, it's just on in the background. It's company, I suppose, especially when Anton is out. Just me, the TV, and Sunny.

Thing is, I hardly ever watch the news. Just doesn't interest me, mostly politics and all that crap. Nothing ever changes, and they mostly do the same stories over and over. I like the crime stories though, and stuff in courts, which is why I pay attention today when I see a copper talking.

It's all about a spate of burglaries that's been happening. The copper says they're looking for information from the public, because some of the burgs were aggravated, and they're worried 'things might escalate'.

Aggravated burglaries are where someone is home when the burg happens, which makes it much worse. This has always seemed a bit strange to me, because it's probably just bad luck if someone happens to be home when burglars come in. Bad luck for both of them, really. But I suppose the courts and police reckon it's worse, because it's more upsetting for the victim, which is probably fair enough.

I don't know where Steve is right now, but Anton is out walking Sunny. When he gets back, I'll tell him what I saw on the news and see what he says. How he reacts.

But Steve gets back before Anton.

And when he comes through the door, I kind of forget about everything – the news, the burglaries, it all disappears. My heart pounds hard. Face goes hot.

He slams the door behind him. Rips off his coat, throws it on the floor.

'That fucking cunt!'

Spits out the words.

My breath goes fast, shallow. Try not to show it.

His eyes bounce all over the place – he paces back and forth in front of the TV. He's ranting in this quiet way, hardly moving his lips, and it makes it seem like there's a volcano underneath.

'Gonna fix that cunt!'

Three times in a row, he says it.

My hands are shaking – can't make them stop. Push them between my thighs. Squeeze them tight. Should say something.

'What happened?'

He stops pacing, glares at me.

'Gave me fuck all. Fifty bucks for all that gear!'

'Jesus,' I say, but have no idea what he's talking about. Safer to go along with it. 'Only fifty bucks?'

Shakes his head. That look again.

'Isn't that what I just said?'

'Yeah,' I say, softly.

'Why repeat it then, ya dumb cunt?'

I really hope Anton will be back soon. But Steve keeps going.

He reckons Emilio doesn't want to take his stuff anymore, because the cops have been round and they know some of it is hot.

'Makes out like he's doing me this huge favour by taking it one last time.'

So Emilio paid pretty much fuck all, even though there were laptops and mobile phones, and even two gold rings.

Steve reckons it was all bullshit about the cops. 'He's just using that as an excuse to talk me down on price. Done it before.'

And there aren't many other places he can go. There are pawnshops around, definitely, but you need ID. And if you don't have ID, they won't take it.

According to Steve, there are two options.

'Either we get some fake ID, or make him pay.'

I'm not sure how he would 'make him', but I keep quiet.

He's doing this thing of squeezing one hand into a fist, then punching the other. Like he's trying to stop himself from hitting something. Or someone.

Emilio was probably telling the truth about the coppers, but it's definitely not the right time to talk about what I saw on the news. Not until Anton has come home.

Apart from anything, I can't be a hundred per cent sure it's them the cops are talking about. Anton never mentioned people being home – he actually said the opposite. They were always careful to make sure no one was there.

Can't think why he'd lie about that.

twenty-one

One week since Anton said it, which means just one week left. It's also the first day I've woken without my face hurting. I still look terrible, but the swelling has almost completely gone, and it's only a bit dark under my eyes.

The problem is my nose, which looks even more bent now without the swelling. I don't think it can be straightened, not completely. Not unless it was by a plastic surgeon or something. And you have to be a millionaire for that.

Even with it bent, I reckon I can still work. I mean, it isn't ideal, but most blokes won't be too bothered. It might rule out a few who like to play boyfriend, but that doesn't happen too often.

Those ones like to kiss and be all affectionate, which I don't really like. It might sound strange, but I prefer the ones who are a bit rough. Not brutal or violent, but who just treat it like a business transaction. It's over pretty quick that way.

But the 'boyfriends', they like to make it last, as though they think I'm enjoying it. They're probably the worst, apart from the pedo ones. Actually, now I think of it, the nose will scare the pedo ones off too. I don't reckon pretending to be their stepdaughter will work so well.

They are seriously so gross. And after they're done, they sometimes ask if I've got kids. That's pretty scary, if you let yourself think about it too much.

But I'll have to get back into it, because I made Anton promise. I made him promise that once we went back to the park, there'd be no more burgs. And I told him what I saw on the news.

'So what?' he said.

'Well, I dunno. Just makes me worry.'

'You think it's us?'

'Dunno.'

He shook his head. 'Just don't worry about it,' he said.

* * *

Anton and Steve must have only just left, because the saucepan is still hot. After breakfast, I'm going to take Sunny out for a walk. I haven't been outside in ages, so I'm looking forward to it.

Victoria Park isn't far from here, which is where Collingwood used to play, but they don't even train there anymore. Not that I'm interested in footy, but it's pretty hard to live in this city without knowing stuff like that, even if you're not interested. Anton knows a bit about footy – 'Mostly by osmosis', he says, but I've never really understood what he meant by that.

I make toast with margarine, which is really delicious. I sit on the couch and eat, and give Sunny some of the crusts. There's some crap on TV about home loans and interest rates. I get a whiff of that chemical smell again, stronger now, and I figure my nose must be getting better.

Steve's door still has the same padlock. Hasn't changed the latch either, and the screws are just the same. I figured he might have made it more secure, seeing as I'd nearly got it open.

But I suppose he reckons what he did was enough to scare me off from doing anything like that again.

* * *

It's when I'm out front that I get the idea. To be honest, I can't believe I didn't think of it before.

I take Sunny back inside and give him a slice of bread. Just a quick look – I've got time for that.

'We'll be going out after.' I scratch his neck. 'You can have a run.'

It's actually still my main plan for the day. This won't take long.

The flat is what some people would call a unit, I suppose. It's red brick and looks uglier every time I see it from the outside. There are two other units along the driveway, but they're all divided by fences. So it's almost like you have your own house, I suppose. I'm guessing someone bulldozed a big old place years ago, built the units, and now collects the rent.

It feels good to be outside in the fresh air, but I don't have time to enjoy the sun. Not yet.

There's a narrow gap down the side of the flat, next to the fence. It looks pretty crappy down there, where the wheelie bins are. I think they haven't been emptied in a while because it stinks something terrible. Even with my nose messed up, it's pretty foul. I suppose none of us have been paying attention to things like that, and there's a fair bit of rubbish on the ground, with flies and torn bags, like maybe rats or crows have gotten into it. I squeeze past the bins and head towards the back end of the flat.

I don't know for sure if it's the right window, but I guess it has to be, because it's near the back corner of the house. The window in my room – Mary's room – faces directly out to the backyard, which is almost as shithouse as down the side of the house, with long weeds and an old clothesline that never gets used.

It must be the right one, but the only problem is it's one of those high windows. Like, one of those ones that are narrow but high up in the wall, so it lets light in, but you can't see your neighbours, and they can't see you. My room at one of my fosters used to have the same, which suited them perfect.

I get the wheelie bin that's most empty, the yellow one, and roll it underneath the window. I can hear Sunny running up and down inside, so I think he must know I'm out here, or maybe he can smell me. Him running up and down like that is making me nervous. I don't know exactly how long Steve and Anton will be, but they're usually out at least till mid-afternoon.

I don't know what to expect – I haven't seen a meth lab before, but I've heard they can be pretty simple. Anton reckons people can make it in car boots or anywhere, and use all sorts of chemicals, which is why he never touches the stuff.

I put one foot against the fence and pull my knees up onto the bin. It takes a fair bit of effort, and it's as wonky as hell, but I manage all the same.

It's a small room, smaller than Mary's one, which probably makes sense seeing as it's her house. There's a single bed, which is tightly and perfectly made with a grey blanket, like it could be one in the army or something. A small, timber cupboard is in one corner, beside the bed. Against the wall, beside the door, are two big black plastic drums.

They're the sort of thing you might normally find in a shed, I suppose – not someone's bedroom. But, to be fair, the flat doesn't have a shed.

So I'm guessing that's where it is – the meth. But there's no tubes or pipes or anything, just the two drums. Both have lids, so whatever is in there must be really strong to still be stinking out the place.

It's his business, I suppose, but I'll definitely tell Anton. It's only one week till we go, but maybe we should leave a bit earlier. Just in case.

There's nothing on the walls, no posters or pictures or anything. It looks like Steve is a full-on neat freak, in his own room at least.

The only other thing out of the ordinary is a box on top of the cupboard, which probably isn't *that* out of the ordinary.

It's one of those old-fashioned hatboxes, the round-shaped ones, which I suppose could be Mary's.

'What you doing?'

A voice behind me – my chest goes tight.

'Hello?'

I turn around.

An old lady. Over the fence. Dressed in black.

'What you do there?'

I climb down slowly. Get a better look.

The neighbour.

'Nothing,' I say. 'Just checking something.'

She frowns. 'Your face. What happen?'

'I tripped.'

Shakes her head, frowns. 'This... this is no good, you know?'

'Was an accident.'

'My husband, he do this too, you see? Is no good.'

Sunny starts barking. 'I better go. Sunny is—'

'He long gone now. Had big stroke, you know?'

I start to wheel the bin back into place.

'You see Maria?'

'Sorry?'

'She come back?'

For a brief moment, I think about telling her – that she's been locked away. At least the old lady might go visit her, which is more than Steve's ever done.

'Ah, not yet. No.'

She nods. 'You tell her, okay? Tell her I ask for her. To come see me, yes?'

I decide that I will tell the old lady, but not till we leave. Maybe I'll leave a note, just so she knows.

* * *

Sunny goes crazy when I get back inside. Jumping on me and licking like I've been away for days.

'Shhh,' I say. 'Good boy.'

Outside, I hear the tinny whine of an engine. Sounds like a motorbike, coming up the driveway.

I pull the curtain slightly aside. Postman. He parks his bike, leaves it running, then comes to the door.

Two quick knocks, then the fly-wire door screeches open. I hear him whistling, tunelessly, then a rustling noise.

A few moments later, the bike revs. I look out again and watch him disappear down the street. I spot the letterbox, number one, overflowing with junk mail.

I loop the rope around Sunny's neck, open the door, and see an envelope placed carefully behind the fly-wire.

Address handwritten.

The first name. Only the first name.

Marietta.

twenty-two

The sun is warm on my skin, but the air is fresh and cool, and it feels good to be outside and away from the flat.

I don't know where Steve and Anton have been walking Sunny, but they mustn't have been taking him far, because he's pulling on the rope like crazy. It's like he's just dying to go somewhere. Anywhere, probably.

Victoria Park is pretty nice, but a bit weird too because it's just an old football ground they've tried to make into a park. I suppose it's good they kept the space though, instead of putting up apartments or whatever.

Anyway, I'd promised Sunny a bit of a run, so I let him off the rope once we're inside the fence. He starts bolting around like crazy and he's completely loving it. He's running up to other dogs too and chasing them around, but he's a bit slow and can't quite catch them.

I take the envelope from out of my back pocket. No surname, so it must be from someone close. Family? A friend?

Marietta.

Smooth, blue ink. Cursive style – a bit old-fashioned.

A crisp, white envelope, not very thick. No return address, no details. A misprinted post office stamp from Hors–am, which I think must be Horsham – a town out west.

Must be her.

Mary or Maria. Whatever she calls herself.

Can't be certain.

I fold it in half, push it back in my pocket.

I know what Anton will say. He'll say you shouldn't open other people's mail. And, to be honest, this looks kind of personal.

Maybe I'll leave it for Mary, for when she gets back. Under her pillow, or somewhere in her room. Somewhere Steve won't see it.

Sunny is getting frustrated, I think. And that's probably why when he does finally catch one of the other dogs, which is one of those skinny whippet things, they have a pretty good blue.

Thing is, I know Sunny looks scary but, like I say, he's actually a major sook. He doesn't usually get into much trouble with other dogs. Anton says he's 'submissive', and Anton knows a bit about dogs, or reckons he does, because he grew up in the country and was a shearer and all that.

Anyway, so I don't know what it is with this whippet thing, but he must have really got under Sunny's skin, because he pins the whippet down and it starts yelping like it's dying. It seems like a bit of an overreaction – a drama queen, from what I can tell.

'Sunny!' I yell, and he looks at me with his tongue out and tail wagging. He lets go of the whippet and bolts across the oval like it's all just a game.

I put the rope back around his neck, but the lady who owns the whippet thing is pretty fired up. She's all Lycra and fleece, and she comes marching over.

'You shouldn't have that sort of dog loose!'

'What's that supposed to mean?'

'What's *what* supposed to mean?'

'What sort of dog?'

'You know,' her lips thin and she spits the words, 'a pit bull.'

'He's not a pit bull. He's a bull terrier. There's a difference.'

She looks me up and down and I can tell what she's

thinking. I can see the wheels turning – 'the penny drops', as Anton says sometimes. She puts her dog on its leash and heads off across the oval. Doesn't say anything else, but I suppose there isn't much else to say.

Normally, when I've got Sunny, people are pretty friendly. It's like having a dog means you can't be a psychopath, or something. People will talk to a complete stranger if that person has a dog with them, but will cross the street to avoid someone on their own.

But if people think you're a junkie, all bets are off – even when you have a dog. My theory is they think you've got nothing to lose. But that's actually not true – you've got more to lose, I reckon. Because when you haven't got much, it means when even small things go wrong, they can seem a lot worse. But when you've got a lot, you can probably ride out the little problems. That's my theory, anyway.

But it's not like I'd trade places with her, or anyone else. I mean, my life obviously isn't perfect, and definitely hasn't been so great lately, but I'm mostly pretty happy. And it's just one week till things get back to normal.

Besides, people who are rich and have nice houses and families and all that are still just people. Like Anton says, you never really know what's going on inside of someone, even if it looks like they're happy, or having a really good life.

The more I think about it, the more I think he's right about that. Because sometimes, even when things might have looked better for me from the outside, the inside of me was much worse. And sometimes it's been completely the other way around.

I reckon that's the same for everyone. Probably.

But out in the sun like this, with just me and Sunny, life is pretty good – not perfect, but pretty good.

'It's all relative,' that's what Anton says. I asked him once what that meant, and he said it means we can only know if we're happy if we compare ourselves to other people. I'm not sure if that's completely true, but probably a little bit.

I'm not a sucker for sob stories or anything like that. For sure, there are people on the street whose lives have been like horror movies. But it's not like every single one has some terrible bad luck, or anything.

I know some people think we're all hard done by. That if we'd gone to a better school, or had better toys, or if Mum and Dad didn't hate each other, we could all be doctors or lawyers or something.

But that just isn't true. And Anton reckons it's almost offensive. He said it tricks people into thinking the world could be fair.

* * *

When I get back to the flat, Anton and Steve still aren't back. I reckon it must be almost five o'clock, and it's starting to get cold. I put on the heater, which is one of those tall grey gas ones, then the TV.

The envelope. It pokes into my skin when I sit down. I take it out, study it, hold it to the light.

If I open it carefully enough, nice and slow, I can seal it back up and she'll never know. But if it's something important, she might need to know right now, so opening it is probably the best thing to do.

That's what I tell myself.

Dear Marietta,
We hope you're well. Your father and I tried to call,
but had no luck.
We are both good, but just need to know you're okay.
Have you heard from Slava? We haven't yet, but
maybe you have.
Anyway, please let us know how you are.
Love,
Mum and Dad

Straight away, I feel bad for opening it. I lick the glue – it's awful and acidic – and re-seal it as best I can. I don't think anyone could possibly tell.

Her parents mustn't know she's been locked up – no one must've told them. To be fair, maybe Steve doesn't know they exist. Some people never talk about their parents, but there's usually a reason for that.

The early news comes on the TV, something about a big car crash on the Western Ring Road, and I wonder whether to tell Anton about the letter. He'll give me a big lecture about it, for sure. But I probably should tell him. Maybe he can bring it up with Steve – not about the letter so much, but just to check whether he knows about her parents.

They probably should be told, one way or another.

And I'm probably pushing my luck a bit to get that photo album out again. But I just want a quick look, mainly to see if there are any pictures of her parents. I turn the TV right down, so I might be able to hear if Steve and Anton are coming back.

There's nothing interesting though – mostly just crappy pics of holiday scenery and some other ones of when she was a kid. I suppose the parents were the ones taking the pictures, so they're never in them.

I find the footy photos again – Steve and Mary and the football scarf. They are the only photos I can find of them together, because the other ones of her are older, like from the 1990s or something, and it looks like she was in a share house somewhere. Most of the pics are her with a bunch of daggy-looking people, like at a house party or something, with smokes and drinks everywhere. I think it was the 90s because of the clothes – all torn jeans, flannel shirts and Doc Martens.

At the back of the album are some more photos of someone who looks a bit like Steve, but much younger. He has his hair gelled right up in a spike, like he thinks he's a punk or something. There are ones of him and two older people, who must be his parents, and one of him playing football when he was a teenager. He was still really skinny, but his skin looks much darker. I guess he got a lot more sun back then – more outdoorsy.

The last one is him at a birthday party. He's sitting behind a table which has got a wrapped present on it, some orange juice in a carton, and what looks like a sponge cake with cream in the middle. I can tell it's his thirteenth, because I count the candles. He's wearing an army helmet and holding a machine-gun, like a soldier's costume or something. He's pointing the gun at the camera. He doesn't look very happy.

Sunny stands up and starts barking like mad. Headlights shine brightly through the curtains – a car coming up the driveway.

I've never seen a car come up there, so I figure it's probably someone visiting the old lady next door. All the same, I close the album. I hear the engine still running – car door slams.

I slide the photo album under the couch cushion. It's just as well, because Steve opens the door right as I do it.

'You're late,' I say, without looking up. I do my best to act casual and change the channel on the TV, like I've been watching it for hours. One of those reality shows about cooking is on.

He shuts the door behind him. I hear the car slowly pull away.

'You got a lift?' I say.

'Taxi.'

'Anton?'

'Had to see someone.'

'Who?'

Steve takes off his coat, drops it on the couch.

'Dunno,' he says. 'But might be a while.'

twenty-three

It's strong.

Maybe strongest I've ever had.

Hard to talk. Makes me think.

That of all the ways.

An overdose wouldn't be so bad.

Like going to sleep.

I'm not suicidal or anything. I know some people get like that when things go bad. Other people are just depressed and that's probably fair enough.

But not me.

Some people might think I'm a likely candidate for the West Gate, but it isn't on my radar. I've got Sunny to look after, for a start.

Plus, I've got Anton.

* * *

I start to straighten up. And I realise Steve has barely said a word the whole time, his breaths slow and deep. Eyes are heavy lidded, swollen looking, with the hint of a smile at the corners of his mouth.

The envelope.

The letter.

Just need to know you're okay.

For a split second, I think about mentioning it – decide not to.

I ask again who Anton went to see.

'Dunno.'

'Didn't say?'

Looks at me. Sighs.

'Someone from inside, I think.'

'Who?'

Shrugs. 'Dunno. But he got moved around the prisons a bit.'

'Anton?'

Nods. 'Only knew him at Barwon. Hostel later on.'

I knew Anton had been in Barwon, but I didn't know they'd been in there together. I wonder why he'd never mentioned it.

I know better than to ask Steve what he'd done to end up there. Anton told me you should never ask what people did to end up in jail, because they never tell you the truth. Not the complete story, anyway.

'Shared a cell for a bit,' he says.

'Yeah?'

'For a while, yeah.'

Steve gets up, puts the stereo on. The volume is low, but it sounds like something British. Radiohead, maybe. I've never really liked them much. He flicks through the tracks, finds the riff he wants.

Lights a smoke, sits back down.

'You know what he did, right?'

I tell him about what happened in the pub, and the girl named Amanda, or Alicia, or whoever she was.

'Got the same story.' He smiles. 'But you know that's all bullshit.'

And he tells me what really happened, which more or less goes like this—

Anton left school pretty young, because he was going to this Catholic place and doing shithouse (which I already knew anyway). But his parents kicked him out, and he got a job as a rouseabout, which was like someone who picks up all the wool off the floors of the woolsheds, and does all the shit jobs.

'Still,' Steve says, 'it meant he had somewhere to stay.'

But the shearers used to pick on him something fierce, which he put up with because he didn't have much choice. 'He'd just cope with it, mostly.' But then, on one of the farms, there was this particular shearer named Bill.

Bill had gone to the same school as Anton. And so he knew about the priest there, and how Anton had been an altar boy.

'So Bill told all the other shearers how Anton was the priest's favourite, right? And it must have really got under his skin, because he went completely bananas one night.'

Smashed Bill with a beer bottle.

'Got his artery. Bled to death well before the ambos got there.'

* * *

It's an awful story. And I think it's worse because of the way Steve tells it – all in one go like that, and with this small smile that makes it seem like he's enjoying it.

I don't know for sure if it's true or not, but it sounds like it could be – it probably makes more sense than the Alicia or Amanda stories. I've got this feeling that it's probably true, or at least partly true.

The music finishes.

'Don't know why he never told me,' I say.

Steve yawns. 'Never told me either. Got the same bullshit. One of the screws filled me in.'

I feel sorry for Anton. I feel sad that he felt like he could never tell me all this time. Like he was ashamed or something, which is terrible. It wasn't his fault, not really. I mean, he probably shouldn't have glassed that bloke, but it was an accident that he died. And it wasn't his fault about the priest, so there was no reason to be ashamed about that.

I'll talk to him about it. Maybe when he gets back from

whoever he's gone to see. After I tell him about the letter. And the meth. Maybe once we're back at the park.

I don't know exactly how I'll bring it up. I'll just have to wait for the right moment.

* * *

I wake up on the couch and the sun is shining all bright and burning my eyes. Sunny is snoring on the floor, and it still must be pretty early.

Steve's door is shut and Mary's is wide open.

It takes a few seconds, but I realise Anton still hasn't come back. I feel nauseous, saliva thick in my mouth.

We always stick together, but especially at night. Since we first started hanging out, I don't think we've spent one night apart.

It's not like we ever talked about it, and it isn't a rule or anything, but I think I've just gotten used to it. Like a family, I suppose – me, him and Sunny. And the more I think about it, the more I feel sick.

I should knock on Steve's door, just to ask him again if he knows anything more about where Anton might have gone, or who he might have gone to see. But it's early, and I don't want to push my luck, especially without Anton around. Steve doesn't seem like a morning person.

I make a piece of toast, but I'm not hungry, and give most of it to Sunny. My head is throbbing, and I could throw up easy, but I can't just sit around and wait. Even though I have no real idea where he is, I'll have to go look for him.

I have this strange feeling I just can't place, but it's not good.

It's not like I believe in being psychic or anything, but I remember Anton once talked about something called 'the collective unconscious'. And it always stuck in my head.

It was in some book he'd read at school. It was something about how there's this whole connection between people, and this power of our brains that we're not even aware of, because it's unconscious.

He explained it better than that, and there's probably a lot more to it, but I think it means sometimes you can know things without actually seeing them, or without being told. Like some kind of extra sense, I suppose.

And that's how I feel about Anton right now, like I can tell he's in some kind of trouble, even though there's nothing to prove it, and no one has told me anything.

I can't explain it.

Can only feel it.

twenty-four

It's really windy at the park. It's nearly always windy, because it's up on a bit of a hill. That's what Anton reckons, anyway.

I could never see any hill, but Anton says it's called Princes Hill, and it's a bit elevated, which is why it gets windy. That's why we'd set up on the east side, behind the grandstand, because he reckoned most of the wind and the weather comes from the west. He said he knew that from when he was a shearer, but I know now that he was actually a rouseabout.

I wonder what else he hasn't told me. He didn't need to lie about that – he didn't need to lie to me about anything.

Sunny is pretty happy to be back at the park. He's sniffing and pissing in all the usual spots, near the bins especially. Someone else has set up in our old position, which is fair enough. It's not a bad set-up – they've got a couple of sleeping bags, some blankets, an old esky, and two of the stripy plastic bags with the zip.

I can't see Anton around, but I'm not that surprised – I just didn't know where else to start. Whoever lives in our spot now isn't there either, but that isn't really so unusual. If people set up somewhere, they don't have to stay and guard it or anything. Other people staying in the park are normally pretty respectful, at least for a day or two, so you can go to the city or whatever you have to do, and still come back home.

That's the thing a lot of people don't understand – it is a

home. It's outside, and sometimes it's cold and wet, but you can still make it comfortable with all your things. Especially if you've got friends there.

Makes me sad, looking at our old spot. I feel this hot sting inside my chest, almost like I want to cry, but I hold it in. And I decide that when I find Anton, I'm gonna say that we should go back right now – not in one week, or even the next day. Apart from the meth or anything else, we just need to get away from the flat and from Steve – so we can get things back to normal.

Stop using so much.

Look to the horizon.

Swim back to shore.

I try to work backwards from Steve coming back to the flat with the gear. I remember on that show, *The Bill*, how the coppers used to work backwards from the scene of a crime. I think that's right.

Steve must have got some money, so him and Anton had probably burged a place. Maybe they got separated after because the owner came home, or something.

Maybe wherever they were doing the burg was far away, and Anton didn't know the way home. He might have gone into the city and crashed at the Salvos for the night. That could be right, I think.

I'm not convinced of it, but it's possible. And it's the best theory I've got.

* * *

I've never regretted having Sunny. At times like this, I realise he's pretty much the only thing I have in the world.

Still, it's a long walk into town, especially after I've already come all the way from Collingwood. My bones ache and I still feel queasy.

Maybe I should go back to the flat first, just to see if he's come back, but I figure if he has, then it won't matter. But if he hasn't, there's no way I can get back into the city before dark.

I go via Lygon Street, because that's the way we used to walk from the park, and I keep my eye out for him the whole way. I even look at the trams going past to see if he's there, just so I don't miss him.

I get to the cemetery, which is about halfway to town, and everything feels so heavy – like I'm moving through something thick. The cemetery bums me out at the best of times, but this time even more than usual. All those dead people.

Anton told me once that the cemetery used to be where the Vic Market is, and then they moved it to Lygon Street. He told me the reason, but I just can't remember.

At the corner of Lygon and Princes Street, just opposite the cemetery, is an old terrace house that Anton said used to be a squat. He reckons he stayed there once. He said it was cold and pretty miserable, and all the trucks thundering past kept him awake. He couldn't wait to get out of there. Princes Street is a really busy road and it goes out to the freeway, which goes out to all these suburbs I've never seen before, and probably never will. I stand with Sunny at the corner and watch the cars and trucks heading out, and I wonder what those people do with their lives. Whether they're going home to their families, or to watch sport, or going for lunch somewhere.

On the side wall of the terrace house, facing Lygon Street, are some old posters and heaps of graffiti. There's one piece of graffiti that Anton said he painted, but I never really believed him. It doesn't look one bit like his handwriting, but then he told me that graffiti was different to handwriting, which is probably true.

THE WORLD IS SICK

That's what it says, and that's all. It's in white capital letters, like someone painted it with a brush and not a spray can. Like they really meant it.

But it's kind of beautiful in its way, just for how plain

and honest and true it is, especially with all those cars and trucks and people going wherever they're going, all day and all night, until one day they just die, and maybe get buried in that cemetery, right there on the same road.

That probably sounds pretty bleak, but it's not how I mean it. I just mean that in the end, it doesn't matter what we do – we all end up the same way.

I stand there with Sunny for a long time, too long, watching the cars go past and thinking of Anton.

And I start to wonder, and not for any particular reason, if Steve has done something to him.

twenty-five

Bull terriers can be really stubborn – if they want to go a particular way, or don't want to walk, they just stop and sit. And if you try to pull them, they lie flat on the ground like an anchor, and it's really hard to get them to move.

And the more I've been pulling Sunny, the more that people are stopping and looking at me.

Normally, I don't care about people staring or anything like that. I don't worry too much about what other people think. But in Lygon Street, I tell one bloke and his footy mates to 'rack off', and another older woman who starts laughing to 'get stuffed'.

And I'm starting to think I really need something. Something soon. Just to take the edge off.

Then one of the restaurant people comes out – I can tell he's like a manager or something, because he isn't dressed like a waiter.

'Clear off,' he says. 'Or I'll call the cops.'

'I'm trying,' I say. 'But Sunny keeps stopping.'

And by the time I get to the Salvos, I must look a bit of a mess. No one's seen Anton, so it was just a complete waste of time anyway. Plus, I get a free lecture from Major Perry.

'Jesus Christ!' he says. 'What happened to you?'

'Nothing. Crap day.'

'There's nothing of you! And who did that to your face?'

'I fell.'

Of course, he knows it's bullshit, but doesn't get angry or anything. He's probably used to people feeding him lies.

I was drunk. I tripped. I fell.

Over the years, he would have heard more lies than people telling the truth, which is pretty shithouse. I mean, I'm not into the churchy side of the Salvos, and they never try to ram that down your throat. But some people on the street treat them like suckers, really. I reckon they must have heard every excuse and every lie you could imagine.

Major Perry perches on the edge of a table, crosses his arms, and sighs in a way that makes him seem about a thousand years old.

'You don't have to tell me. But I can get you a bed if you need, you know? No cops or anything.'

He's pretty smart, Major Perry. He must think it's Anton who did it, and he knows I'll never dob him in. To be honest, it's a pretty good offer. But it's hard to think about properly right now. It's hard to think about anything, because I'm getting a craving something fierce.

'Nah, I'm fine.'

'Really?' He raises his eyebrows, looks me up and down, which isn't very subtle.

'Yeah. And I've got Sunny, remember?'

'Sunny?'

'My dog. And he's tied up out front, so I better get moving. But if you see Anton, let him know I'm looking for him, okay?'

He nods. 'Offer's always here, all right?'

'Right.'

He reaches over and squeezes my shoulder.

'Try to look after yourself, okay?'

I shrug.

'Yep.'

* * *

Steve looks pretty relaxed. He's sitting on the couch, watching TV, which I hardly ever see him do.

Maybe he thinks he's too intellectual or something. Like he's too smart for it. Or that's what he wants people to think.

'Anton?' I say.

'What?'

'Been back?'

Steve shrugs. 'Not since I've been here.'

He's watching a show about antiques or some crap. Some old lady is getting a painting valued and says how she's over the moon.

'You score?' I say.

He doesn't lift his gaze from the TV. 'Got any cash?'

That pisses me off a bit. Maybe more than a bit.

It seems cold to say it, but even though I'm worried about Anton, I need to make sure we've got some gear. It's non-negotiable. I already feel so utterly shit and hollowed out – it's only gonna get worse.

The ads come on, and Steve looks at me. He stares for a bit, frowns, almost like he's trying to make his mind up about something. But maybe I'm imagining it.

'Not gonna be doing any burgs for a while,' he says. 'Keeping a low profile.' He reaches into his pocket and pulls out a baggie. 'Won't be as much to go round, you know? But this one is on the house.'

He slides it across the coffee table. I snatch it. Cool relief flows through me.

'Actually, on second thoughts, it's on credit.'

The antiques show finishes. Steve switches off the TV, gets up.

'Not having any?' I say.

'Nah,' he says. 'All yours.'

He goes to his room and shuts the door behind him. I can see he's turned the light on inside, and I wonder what he's doing. Maybe he's having the meth instead – could be his new thing.

I sit on the floor with Sunny and he gives my face a lick. There's nothing I can do about Anton right now. I'll worry about that tomorrow. Tomorrow, I'll go out and find him, and we can start to get everything back to normal. Back to the park and how things were.

Anton won't agree right away, but I'll convince him it's the right thing to do. We won't even have to tell Steve. Will probably be better if he doesn't know where we are. Things will get back to normal soon.

I try hard to convince myself.

But I have something that makes it easier. Much easier. Can believe almost anything then – that's just one of the things that's great about it.

But it also lets you forget about things too.

I hear Steve in his room, and I wonder what he's laughing at. Must have thought of something funny. Or maybe it's the meth kicking in.

That must be it, I decide.

twenty-six

People talk about seeing a light when you die. Like, they're in a tunnel or something. Travelling towards the light.

I think religious people believe it more than most, from what I've seen on TV. They have those near-death experiences, where they almost die, but are revived and come back. It's a bit ridiculous really.

It's surprising what people believe in sometimes. Like, I remember this stupid show I watched years ago. It was back when I was with some fosters who pretended to be all churchy. I say 'pretended' because what they did in the bedroom wasn't very churchy. All a bit of an act, as far as I could tell.

Anyway, this show was called *Highway to Heaven* and it was about this angel who was kind of on probation before he could get into Heaven. So he gets sent down to Earth to prove himself by doing good deeds all round the place.

It was all old repeats, and just so ridiculous. But my foster brother, he actually thought it was a true story. I think he thought it was some kind of documentary. Which I guess proved to me pretty early on that some people will believe almost anything.

Anyway, there's a reason why I mention it – this thing about seeing the light. I never believed in any of that, because everyone knows it's make-believe, right? Anton used to say sometimes that it's just a way to make people whose life is crap accept it, because things will be better when you get to Heaven. He reckoned it was mostly just to stop poor people from robbing rich people. Something about a camel and a needle. He put it better than that, but you get the drift.

It was never an issue for me anyway. He was preaching to the converted, I told him, which he thought was funny. I knew there was no Heaven and no Hell. There was definitely no God, and there was no Devil either.

But if you were going to believe in anything, I'm happier to believe in the Devil. He's just a much more interesting character, I suppose. And more believable, because he's more like people are on Earth. I mean, there are more people doing bad shit than there are people who are like God, or like angels floating around in clouds.

What do angels even do, anyway, apart from sit around? It all looks pretty boring, if you think about it. At least in Hell, things would be interesting. And I'd probably know more people there, if there was such a place, which I don't believe in anyway. It makes me think of this movie I saw once. It was one of the times me and Anton snuck into the cinema. It was completely by chance, because we didn't know what was on, but it turned out to be one of my favourite movies ever. It was called *Breaking the Waves* and we missed the first bit, but it was about this woman whose husband gets paralysed in an accident. She lives on an island and basically has sex with as many men as she can. She does it to try to save her husband, so he'll be able to walk again. Kind of like some weird sacrifice, I suppose.

I know that all probably sounds ridiculous, and I'm not explaining it very well. But it's honestly one of the most beautiful movies you could ever see.

It's a love story, which I don't normally believe in either. And I don't want to give away what happens, in case you haven't seen it, but it ends with these big iron bells ringing up in Heaven.

And that's probably how I imagine it will be, I think, if

there actually could be such a place, and if I could ever get to see it.

* * *

It's a bit of a surprise to see the light. It's round and white and so incredibly bright. It starts off small, but seems to be getting bigger. It's like I'm moving closer to it, or maybe it's moving closer to me.

Maybe it's a dream and I'm asleep. Do you actually think when you're having dreams? I'm not sure. Maybe you're just supposed to remember them afterwards.

But the light is definitely getting bigger and brighter. It's forcing out all the darkness and I feel pretty good, like it's a good thing that's happening. Like the light is gonna take me somewhere pretty sweet. Somewhere special. Somewhere I've never been. Away from Steve, the flat, and any of this.

I can almost believe it.

* * *

The light. The light keeps growing. And I'm feeling better and better, the bigger it gets.

I open my eyes. Slowly. *So bright.*

'Hello, can you hear me? Hello?'

Indian voice. Something like that. It's warm and smooth like velvet.

'Can you hear me? Hello?'

So tired. Like never before in my life.

'Stay awake now.'

The brightness.

'I want you to keep your eyes open for me. I want you to stay awake. Do you understand?'

Yes.

'Do you know where you are?'

No.

'You are in hospital. You are in St Vincent's Hospital. Do you understand?'

I understand.

'I am Doctor Ashish. I am one of the consultants. Do you know why you are here?'

No.

'Are you a drug user?'

Yes.

'Keep your eyes open, okay?'

Okay.

'Are you a heroin user?'

Sometimes.

'Do you know what has happened?'

No.

'You are very lucky.'

Yes.

'But you need to keep your eyes open. For me, okay?'

Okay.

'Don't cry.'

No.

'You are going to be all right. I promise.'

twenty-seven

I sleep for a long time.

Maybe it's because I haven't been getting much sleep, or maybe they gave me something. I don't know.

When I wake, I have a tube in my arm.

I hear someone, a woman.

'Dehydrated.'

I think they're putting other stuff in the drip too. That's fine by me.

The bed is firm and the sheets feel so clean.

Even though the hospital is noisy and bright, I sleep deeply. When I wake, all I want is to sleep again.

Then, a soft voice.

'Okay?'

I open my eyes but there's no doctor, no nurse. I have a metallic taste on my tongue. Mouth dry and sticky.

'Water?' I say.

'*Si, si.*'

The soft, small voice beside the bed. I turn – it's an old woman. Thick glasses and curly hair – a silver chain. She fills a small plastic cup from a jug.

'You drink,' she says. She stands and helps it to my mouth. I cough. She sits back down. '*Scusa,*' she says.

I shuffle my legs up under the blanket. They hurt. Ache. My stomach too. I turn to her.

She smiles a little. Gold in her teeth. Necklace. A crucifix.

'You remember?'

'No.'

'You no remember?'

'No.'

I close my eyes.

'We talk before. I come to door. You no remember?'

'I... no.'

'You Maria's friend?'

'Maria?'

'Then yesterday, *o Dio mio!*'

'Yesterday?'

'*Si*, yesterday. Very early. Still dark. You really no remember?'

'No.'

'I explain to you now then. You see, I come home very late. From the casino, with my *sorella* and I—'

'Sorella?'

'*Scusa*, my sister. Assunta. She big gambler, you know? Especially since husband die. Now, she got his super. So pokies, you see?'

I nod.

'I no play, just sit with her. For company, you know? And I come home with the taxi.'

I open my eyes.

Attention all staff: Code grey. Code grey. Level three, cubicle two. Two security men dressed in black rush past.

'So I come home with the taxi, and you outside. You are in the gutter, you see?'

I swallow. My throat clicks drily.

'At first, I think you looking for something. Maybe something you drop? But then I see you were, how you say?'

'Water, please?'

'*Si, si.*' She fills my cup. 'So you were... ah, unconscious. So I get taxi, the man, I get him to call ambulance, okay? That's why you are here, no?'

I drink the water. It's cool and delicious.

'The doctors here. They say you very lucky. *Very lucky.* They say with these drugs, you might never wake up.'

Attention all staff: All clear, code grey. Level three, cubicle two. All clear.

'Big overdose. Very bad.'

I nod.

'These drugs, these are no good for you, yes?'

'Yes.'

'I tell that man, the tall man. I tell him what happened.'

'Who?'

'The tall man. Maria's friend. I tell him you here. But he not come, you know? I say to him, tell Maria then. And you know what he do?'

The security men walk past this time. There's a scream somewhere on the ward. One of them smiles.

'He laugh like crazy person.' She shakes her head. 'Something is wrong with him, I think.'

I nod.

'So I come.'

'Yes.'

A machine beeps somewhere behind the curtain. A nurse walks past, turns to me, smiles gently. The old lady takes my cup.

'More?'

'No.'

'You have family?'

'No.'

'You tell me, I call them.'

'No family.'

'No one?'

'Just Anton. Sunny.'

'Who?'

'Anton's a friend. Sunny's my dog. Have you seen them?'

She frowns. 'Where?'

'Mary's. Maria's, I mean.'

Shakes her head, 'No, I'm sorry.'

'Doesn't matter,' I say.

* * *

When I tell the nurse I want to leave, she gets all funny. Says I'll have to wait till the doctor sees me.

Thing is, I'm feeling much better. I've been here maybe three days now, and the rest has done me good.

It's not that the nurses and doctors and everything aren't really nice. Even the orderlies.

I'm sure they all know why I'm here, but they still treat me good. Like a normal person, I suppose. I'm not really used to that.

One of the orderlies, an older bloke with faded green tattoos, he's probably the most friendly.

'Overdid it, did ya?' Grins like a cat. Busted teeth.

'I... I suppose, yeah.'

He leans in and rubs my shoulder.

'Been there, done that. Bought the t-shirt.' Laughs, breath like mouthwash. 'Don't make a habit of it, though. Ending up in this place, I mean.'

I nod. Force a smile.

Truth is, I don't really remember any of it – what happened, I mean. I don't remember shooting up, or going outside, or anything.

It's weird that I'd go outside, but I try not to think about it too much. I mean, sometimes you do strange things when you're on it.

* * *

The old lady from next door comes back again. She brings lasagne, which one of the nurses heats up. It's delicious and warm inside me – I feel better for it.

'Is okay?'

'Lovely.'

She doesn't sit down. 'You come back?'

'Sorry?'

'To Maria's. You come?'

'Maybe.'

'You tell Maria then? You tell her come see me, okay? When you see her.'

I remember the letter. Her parents. Too much to tell right now.

'Okay,' I say.

I still have to find Anton. I even got one of the nurses to look up his name, to see if maybe he'd been at the hospital. Nothing.

Once I get out, I'll ask Dirty Doug, because the cops might know. I'll get a big lecture for my trouble, but I'm used to it. And it's probably fair enough this time.

But first, before any of that, I need to make sure Sunny is okay. I figure Steve probably would have just left him alone, but I don't know if he would have refilled his water bowl, or given him enough food.

Besides, maybe Anton is back by now. Maybe Anton is back and it can be me and him and Sunny again.

To be honest, if it wasn't for Sunny and Anton, I'd be happy to stay in the hospital a while longer. I mean, you get looked after pretty well, served meals and drinks, and there's a little TV above the bed, which is okay to pass the time, even if there's mostly crap on.

I saw a crime story on the news that was a bit of a shock, though. A murder in Fitzroy – second-hand dealer. When they showed the place, I realised I knew whose house it was – Emilio's.

He'd been 'stabbed multiple times,' the copper said, and 'couldn't be revived,' and he 'died at the scene.' They reckoned it was 'a senseless crime, in broad daylight,' and the police were looking for information from the public.

Even if Emilio was a bit of a creep, and he was stingy as hell, he probably didn't have that coming.

* * *

A young woman comes to see me. She's kind of pretty, with hair like a pixie. She steps in close beside the bed, bit nervous-like.

'Hello,' she says, too brightly. 'I'm Peta, one of the social workers here. Just hoping to have a quick chat.'

I'll spare you the details, because I've heard this kind of thing plenty of times before. To be honest, it isn't my first time in hospital, so I know the routine. She asks if I have somewhere to stay, how long I've been using, and if I'd tried any rehab services. The usual.

'Try to think of this like an opportunity. A chance to reset, get some change happening.'

She's nice, don't get me wrong, but I don't think she really understands. I mean, some people think that your life can be fixed with a bit of counselling, and then it's all happy days.

But that's the last thing I need. I don't need to talk about the past, or even think about it. I just need to find Anton and then look forwards, you know? Get back to the park. Use a bit less. Start to change things.

Counselling and that kind of stuff probably works for some people, maybe. But it's not really my thing.

'I'll give you my card anyway,' she says. 'And the doctor still wants to see you.'

It's probably the worst part of being in the hospital, I think the waiting. You're always waiting for something – food, X-rays, blood tests, whatever. I suppose I could just get up and leave, but I kind of like that Indian doctor. Not in a romantic way or anything. I don't like anyone in a romantic way, really. But there's something nice about Doctor Ashish. Something real.

He has this gentle way of talking, like he treats you with respect. And it makes me kind of respect him too, I suppose. So I don't want to disappoint him by just running off. Normally, I would figure that the doctors and nurses wouldn't care anyway. St Vincent's is a crazy busy place, and they've probably got twenty people out there waiting for my bed.

He's pretty nice though, not like the doctors in hospital normally are. They're usually different than regular ones – a bit distant, if you know what I mean. I guess they see a lot of crap every day and it makes them a bit jaded, or something. Like coppers, I suppose.

'I hear you want to leave us.'

He sits on the edge of the bed, checks his clipboard, frowns, then places it down. Aftershave. Like the park after rain. Earthy, but sweeter.

'Got things to do, you know? My dog and my friend Anton he—'

'This your first overdose?'

'First one like this.'

He crosses his arms. 'I think you should stay a little longer.'

'Why?'

'I know you say it... that this was an accident?'

'Yeah... I mean, must have been. I don't really remember.'

He leans back and pulls the curtains closed behind him.

'I am concerned...' He hesitates, can see him searching for the right words. 'I'm concerned you could be a risk.'

I realise where he's going. 'What do you mean?'

'To yourself.'

'I'd never do that. It's just not... you know, I've been through some bad stuff, but never that.'

He smiles, but it's the sort of knowing smile people do. It's like when they think they can see through what you're saying. When they think they know the truth.

'The previous episodes?' he says.

'Episodes?'

'Your stays in hospital. Involuntary. I've seen your record and—'

A woman laughs loudly out on the ward. Footsteps pass heavily behind the curtain.

'I'm over all that now.'

He does that smile again.

'Listen, I want to be straight with you. We are not seeing heroin overdoses at the moment.'

'So?'

'Well, if purity is high, we see them. Many of them. But you are an experienced user, which is... that's why it rings alarm bells, you see?'

I can understand what he means. It doesn't really make sense – I'm always careful with that sort of thing. Really careful.

'I must have made a mistake.'

He looks at me in the eyes for a long time – too long.

'We found Oxycodone in your blood. A high level. You must have taken a big dose.'

'Oxy...?'

'Like Endone? You take this?'

'No... just a bit a little while ago, but not now.'

'Mixed with heroin, it's dangerous. Depresses your central nervous system. Understand?'

Endone? It doesn't make sense.

'I can't stop you from leaving, but I am going to give you a referral. For a rehab program. Residential.'

'I can't—'

'It would be in your best interests. But you don't have to decide right away.'

He hands me an envelope. Smiles, properly this time.

'I cannot make you. No one can. But at least you'll have it, you know?'

He touches my shoulder, gently.

'For when you are ready.'

twenty-eight

The front desk lady is lovely. She offers to call a taxi, but I really want to walk. It feels like ages since I've been outside. Doctor Ashish gave me some pills to help with withdrawal, and he says I should try to stay on them as long as I can.

'But if you start using again, stop the pills right away.'

It's probably the most likely outcome – at least for now – and I reckon the doctor knows it too, because he didn't bother with a repeat prescription. I always check things like that. And the packet only has ten tablets in it, even though the box says there's supposed to be twenty.

I've got a bit of time to think about things. Usually, that's easier when I'm walking. Part of me is dreading going back to the flat – maybe most of me – but there isn't really much choice.

And a small part of me is hopeful too. It's so long since I've seen Anton, and maybe he's back by now. Maybe I won't need to go ask Dirty Doug for help. For a few minutes, I let myself believe it – and it gives me this warm feeling inside. It'll be really great to see him.

Plus, I've missed Sunny something fierce. Even just these couple of nights – it's the longest we've ever been apart.

I know I can always rely on Sunny. He'll always be there. Even when I act like a dick or screw things up, he doesn't care. It's pretty hard to find people like that. Maybe impossible.

Dogs love you no matter what. And they love the real, naked you – not just the show you put on for other people.

They're probably better at being human than any of us really. Maybe they learned over time from watching us, and became expert at doing the best bits. The bits about love.

* * *

It's almost dusk by the time I get back.

I knock, but no answer.

Still have the key.

All the same, I check round the side first. The windows are dark, but someone might still be home, so I knock again.

Nothing.

Mary might have come back from the psych hospital – that worries me a bit. Not so much because I'll get kicked out of her room, which is fair enough, but I'm worried Anton and Sunny might have already left, and then I'll have to go look for them. That doesn't sound very appealing, especially at night.

I open the door slowly, and the smell hits me straight away – worse now. Putrid, thick – almost unbearable.

'Hello?'

I go in as quietly as I can – don't want to freak anyone out. Especially if Mary's there.

'Hello?' I say again.

I close the door carefully behind me. The smell is rich, sickening – saliva fills my mouth. I reach for the light switch beside the door, but I can't remember which side it is. I slide my hand up and down the wall, but then I sense something moving in the room.

I stop breathing.

And footsteps rush towards me through the darkness.

* * *

It's probably the closest I've ever come to having a heart attack.

Sunny!

He goes crazy, jumping up and licking me like he's never done before.

'Good boy! Good boy!'

I find the light switch – the lounge and kitchen are empty. Mary's door is shut, Steve's is locked.

I call out again, just to be safe.

'Anyone home?'

No answer. Mary mustn't have come back yet, and Steve is out doing whatever he's doing.

Maybe Anton is with him.

* * *

It must be after midnight. I've had about half the packet of pills, which isn't that smart. The TV's on, but the light's off, so it's hard to see who it is.

'Anton?' I say. I'm a bit woozy.

No answer. Sunny sits up and whines.

'That you?'

The door closes. The light's still off.

'What are you doing here?'

Steve.

'Where's Anton?' I say.

'How should I know?'

He walks into the kitchen, opens the fridge and gets himself a beer. I see his face in the fridge light, all pale skin and sharp cheekbones.

He cracks the top off his beer and leans back against the bench. I want to get up and turn the light on, but don't know if he wants that. And there's something about the way he's standing there, the angle of him, drinking the beer and looking at me – it's making me nervous.

Rage is on the TV. Bowie. 'Young Americans'.

'Thought you were dead.'

I see his thin smile in the blue-grey light from the TV, and I'm kind of relieved. He's one of those people where you grab hold of whatever you can, whatever little sign or hint they might be normal, or human.

That probably doesn't sound like much of a compliment.

Maybe because it isn't.

twenty-nine

There's a small reception room, with a desk and a door behind it. A big window too – it's one of those reflective ones where you can't see in, but they can see out. I think nearly all the stations have them.

I've been waiting at the desk for ages. It's felt like ages anyway, and no one has come out from behind that glass. I wonder if they're just waiting for me to leave or something, but there's no way I'm going. Not after I've come all this way. Not till I've seen Dirty Doug.

I've been worried about Sunny pretty much the whole time – imagining someone untying his rope, and walking off with him down the street.

I think it's like that when you really love someone – it's the same as loving a dog. Every time you see them, you're almost surprised they're there. It's like you don't deserve it, and that any minute now they might be gone. That's how I feel about Sunny, anyway.

If Dirty Doug is behind that glass, he would have definitely come out by now. But I don't really know where to find Dirty Doug, which station I mean. Thing is, he always finds me, not the other way around.

I figured he must be from one of the city stations. This is the closest one – in Flinders Lane, just near Swanston. Even if he doesn't work here, I reckon they'll be able to look him up on their computer system. Help me find him.

I need to know if he's seen Anton around. Or maybe he might be able to help look for him. He'd have some ideas about how to find him, definitely. Cops do stuff like that all the time, looking for missing people, so there must be some sort of procedure, some sort of process they follow. It's something they would get trained for, I reckon.

Dirty Doug will help me for sure. But these coppers, hiding behind that glass, they probably just think I'm some junkie.

I'm close to walking out when the door finally opens – a young copper with blond hair and a broad face. He must've got the short straw. He has tattoos on his arms, which I think's a bit weird, but I suppose you're allowed to do that nowadays. His nametag says he's a constable – Constable McLeod – and I decide to be polite.

'Hello Constable.'

He nods. Doesn't answer.

He stays behind the counter with his arms crossed, and the blank copper 'no-face', which I'm sure they must teach at the academy. They must have whole classes on how to do it, and how to look like you couldn't give a shit about anyone. They probably test you on it, and I reckon you must get kicked out if you fail, because I don't think I've ever seen a copper who hasn't got it in their repertoire. I've even seen Dirty Doug do it to people, and he's about the nicest copper there is.

'I'm looking for one of your colleagues.'

'Yeah?'

'Yeah.'

'What for?'

'He's a friend.'

Constable McLeod gets this little smile.

'That right?'

'His name's Doug.'

'Doug?'

I can't remember Doug's surname, but I think it starts with M. Mallard maybe? Can't be sure.

'Doug,' I say. 'Or maybe Douglas.'

'Got that. No Doug here. Or Douglas. Anything else?'

'Well, I —'

He turns to go back behind the mirror where you can't see anything.

'Wait. Some people call him Dirty Doug.'

He frowns.

'Can't you look it up?' I say.

'Look what up?'

'His name.'

He shakes his head. 'Whose name?'

'Doug.'

I can hear laughing. It's coming from behind the glass where I can't see, and Constable McLeod gets that little smile back, and I realise what's going on.

Now, a lot of people might tell him and his mates to go get fucked at this point. But I know better than that.

It's no good to argue with coppers, or get abusive, even if they're treating you like crap. Only makes things worse.

'Thanks a lot,' I say.

* * *

The copper has gotten me so fired up that I start walking down the street and almost completely forget about Sunny.

Still, he doesn't realise. He wags his tail and I lean down and let him lick my face. I give him a really good pat, and I try not to think about Constable McLeod.

Need to stay focused.

I'll have to try one of the other stations, even though I'll probably get similar treatment. In a way, I sort of understand. I mean, I don't look that crash hot, and – from what Dirty Doug tells me – most coppers are keen to avoid work whenever they can. If they think you're a junkie, or a bit rough around the edges, you don't have much hope really.

There's another station on Spencer Street, I think, but that's a fair hike. So first, I might go to the Salvos again, just to see if Anton has been there since last week. Plus, I'm pretty hungry. There was no bread at the flat, and I can probably score me and Sunny a feed.

Being in hospital, I got a bit spoilt with meals and that. And I've kind of got my appetite back, which is probably a good thing.

* * *

It's pretty empty, which is usually the case around mid-morning. If you come too early, you get the ones who have been up all night and are strung out – can get a bit dangerous. But now's a pretty good time – a couple of old blokes drinking coffee, noses in the form guide. Probably no money to bet on anything, just old habits.

I'm about halfway through some bacon and eggs, which are delicious, when Major Perry sits down opposite me. It's a big table, and there are plenty of empty spaces, but I don't say anything.

'You're looking better,' he says.

'Better than what?'

It comes out harsher than I meant.

'Last time I saw you.'

I swallow what's in my mouth.

'Sorry. Thanks.'

He clears his throat. 'I heard the news.'

'What news?'

He frowns, shakes his head as though he misheard me.

'Anton.'

'What about him?'

'You haven't...' he trails off, eyes searching mine.

He takes off his glasses, which I've never seen him do.

He has those ones that tint in bright sunlight, which are pretty daggy, and they go dark under the fluoro lights in here too.

He's actually kind of nice looking, in this really white-bread way. A bit pudgy, but gentle eyes. Safe.

'Anton,' he says again.

I put down my knife and fork – they clink too noisily against the plate.

'What about him?'

He folds his glasses and puts them down carefully on the table. He fiddles with the frame, the hinges. He studies them like they're suddenly very important.

'He... um...'

'What?'

Major Perry raises his gaze, meets mine directly.

'A... a robbery gone wrong. That's what they're saying. At a pawnshop.' He squints. 'You really didn't hear?'

It takes a while to process. I think part of me doesn't want to make the connection – not right away – but he makes it clear.

'Murder,' he says. 'They want Anton for murder.'

They kind of hang in the air, those words. Echo somehow, like everything and everyone else has gone quiet.

'There's footage of him out on the street. CCTV. Running from the scene.' He puts his glasses back on. 'Heard it was on the news last night.'

I grasp the edge of the table. Try to breathe.

'I'm sorry,' he says. 'I know you two are good friends.'

The bacon and eggs swirl in my belly. I might throw up. *It just can't be...*

But the first thing I think of isn't about Anton. It's Major Perry.

I decide I'll know for next time. I'll be ready.

If he ever takes those glasses off, he has really bad news. He has something just awful to tell me.

thirty

It just doesn't make sense.

I mean, Anton glassed that bloke once, which had got him in jail over that girl, or the priest, or whatever. But, apart from that, he doesn't have a violent bone in him.

The more I think about it, the more I'm sure they must have got it wrong – there's no way Anton would have done it.

'Things must have got out of hand.'

That's what Major Perry said.

Got out of hand.

It was like he just accepted it to be true, even though Anton has always been really polite to Major Perry. It's like none of that counts for anything. Like who you are, or how you behave – your character – none of it means a thing. And all because of something the cops said about what they saw on CCTV.

It really pisses me off.

I'm angry at Major Perry, but I'm more angry at Steve. He must've known, but didn't tell me. He didn't tell me anything.

* * *

I've been watching game shows and crap TV and pacing the room for what feels like forever.

I hear his key in the lock. He steps in, switches on the light. Sunny stands up, like he feels what I'm feeling.

'Hey,' he says. Stays in the doorway.

I see him twitch, lips and eyes, then it disappears. Like he's annoyed to see me, but tries to hide it.

I don't really know exactly what to say, or where to start. I probably should have thought about it, planned it better.

'I know what happened.'

He closes the door behind him, heads for the kitchen.

'What are you on about?'

'Anton.'

He opens the fridge, takes out a beer. 'What did you hear?'

I turn off the TV, then tell him what Major Perry said.

He cracks open the bottle, takes a long drink.

'So?'

'Is it true?'

He nods.

'Why didn't you tell me?'

Shrugs. 'Must've forgotten.'

'Did you...'

'What?'

'Were you there?'

He hesitates, almost like he's deciding what to tell me.

'Yeah. Split right after. He must've got spotted.'

Steve finishes his beer quick. Gets another.

'Want one?'

'Okay,' I say, even though I don't.

He brings me the beer, sits down on the couch.

'Why don't you sit?' he says.

'I'm right.'

'Suit yourself.'

And he reckons it happened something like this –

'After we scored some gear, we went to Emilio's to ask for more money. Like I said, the cunt's been ripping us off pretty bad. I didn't really think we'd have much luck, but I figured at least he might pay more next time.

'So we confronted him. Then he gets all pissed off and tells us that if we don't like it, we can take our stuff somewhere else. And that's when it all kicked off.

'Anton just starts going bananas, like I've never seen before – smashing stuff in the shop. So Emilio picks up this steel bar from under the counter, but Anton's quick and grabs it too. And next thing Anton is on top of him.

'He only hit him twice. But his head just kind of caved in, eyes rolled back to the whites. Must've had a thin skull or something. Blood everywhere. Knew right away he was fucked.

'So we both took off in opposite directions. Anton had a lot of blood on him, so it was no good to be together.

'I ran towards the Edinburgh Gardens, but I didn't really know where Anton was headed. And that was the last time I saw him, until I saw it on the news. And the worst bit was he had the gear too, which is a bit of a shit.'

Steve tells me all this almost like he's talking about the weather. Like, he's just really matter-of-fact about it, like it was the most everyday thing to bash someone to death with a steel bar. And everyone should just carry on like normal.

'Cops came round here too, looking for him. While you were in hospital.' He sips at his beer. 'I've gotta stay under the radar. No more burgs or anything for a while.'

Thing is, the way Steve tells the story, it's almost believable. I mean, I never thought Anton could be so violent, but I suppose that's what got him in jail in the first place – a rush of hot temper. Still, something doesn't sit right.

He finishes his beer. I haven't even started mine. He puts the TV back on – some show about forensic police or something. Looks terrible.

'Know where he is?' I say.

'Nah.' Turns up the volume. 'Could be interstate by now.'

'Right.'

Cocks one eyebrow. 'You planning on finding him?'

'Maybe.'

'Don't. Cops'll be watching.' He clunks his empty down

on the coffee table. 'I don't want any hint of him coming back here, right?'

I nod.

'Last thing I need is pigs sniffing around.'

Maybe it's that word, 'sniffing'. Maybe that's what finally makes me ask.

'Is it... because of the smell?'

He gives me that look.

'What?'

'The chemical smell. Is it meth?'

He eyes me for a while, like he's thinking about what I've said. Or maybe like he's trying to read my thoughts. I shift my feet, look away.

Sunny whines – he might be hungry.

Steve smiles, doesn't answer.

'Drink up,' he says. 'Just beers tonight.' He stands and heads for the fridge. 'Might score something tomorrow, I reckon.'

I sit down on the couch, take a sip of the beer. It's warm and disgusting. He gets himself another from the fridge and flips the top onto the floor.

'Got family?' he says.

'Anton?'

'Nah, you.'

'Nah, not really. Why?'

He shrugs. 'Just wondering. Making conversation, you know?' He sits down and clinks his beer against mine. 'Cheers right? Me and you then, for a bit.'

'Cheers.' I take a deeper drink.

I'm not going to stick around though, not without Anton. But I don't think it's the best time to say it – I'll wait for a bit, maybe tomorrow. Then I'll tell him.

Or maybe just leave without saying.

thirty-one

Slept terribly, thinking about Anton.

Sweats.

Aching arms and legs.

Steve is already up and in the kitchen.

'Breakfast?' he says, too brightly. Drops a slice of bread in the toaster before I answer.

I squat down and give Sunny a good pat.

'Just thinking,' he says, 'might have a crack at begging today.'

I stand up too quick. Dizzy.

'You?'

'Yeah. Might take Sunny and give it a go.'

I can't really imagine Steve begging. Too proud, like it's beneath him.

But if it means he'll be able to score, that's a good thing – if I feel sick now, it's only going to be worse by tonight. Then I'll leave first thing tomorrow. Definitely.

Plus, if Steve's occupied, it will give me more time to find Dirty Doug. Set things straight.

'Be careful, yeah?'

Toast pops up. It's a bit burnt, but I don't mind it like that.

'Careful?' he says. He drops the toast on a plate for me.

'Sunny. Don't lose him.'

Doesn't answer.

I give Sunny another pat and a scratch on his back, and I tell him to be a good boy. I nuzzle into him, which I know he likes.

Steve ties the rope around his neck a bit too tight, but I don't say anything. Still, I reckon he sees it in my eyes.

'We'll be right,' he says. 'Don't worry.'

* * *

After Steve leaves, I decide to have another piece of toast. Sometimes little decisions like that, which usually mean nothing, can make a big difference. Not very often, but sometimes.

Me and Anton saw a movie about it once – it was a romantic one and was mostly crap. It was an older movie they showed again especially for Valentine's Day. It had Gwyneth Paltrow in it, I think, and I'm not really into that sort of stuff. I've never really understood why some directors feel like they need happy endings – it always seems really fake. It's like they just don't want to upset people, or show what life is really like. Like it's all about money.

Anton told me once that in Hollywood they 'workshop' endings, which is when they make all these different endings for a movie and show them to audiences to see which is the most popular. It seems like a strange way to do it, because being popular doesn't make it good, I don't think.

There's no Vegemite or jam left, but there's margarine, which is actually really delicious on its own. Steve has had the last of the coffee, but I find a teabag and wait extra long to make it stronger. And that's when there's a really loud knock at the door.

Whack! Whack!

My heart races – Anton.

But could be the neighbour, the old lady. She might have seen Steve leave and decided to check on me.

Or might be Mary.

Maybe I shouldn't answer. Maybe I should just wait and—

Whack! Whack! Whack!

What could I tell her? It would have to be the truth. I mean, I haven't really done anything wrong – Steve invited us to stay, so it's not like we've been squatting or anything. And I could give her the letter from her parents. She won't know I've opened it, so it should be fine. That might make her—

Whack! Whack! Whack!

I just don't want to open the door.

Then, I see a shadow moving behind the thin, white curtain of the window, beside the door – she isn't going to give up.

'Coming,' I say.

The whole thing with Anton and Steve and Emilio is too much to explain. But I'll make a move as quick as I can – today, once I get Sunny back. Dole payment is in a couple of days, and I can get a new sleeping bag and head for the park. That'll be for the best really. And Anton will know where to find me.

In the meantime, I can go see Major Perry and see if one of the hostels might take me and Sunny for a couple of nights. He'll look after me, I think.

Deep breath.

Open the door.

But it isn't Mary – it's two coppers.

A man, and a skinny woman with a dark blue folder.

'Afternoon,' the man says.

I eye them both, looking for some hint.

'This about Anton?' I say.

She's the one who speaks. 'Marietta?'

Both of them look at me a bit uncertain. He glances at her, frowns, shakes his head.

'She's not here,' I say.

Bloke says, 'Know where she is?'

He's tall and slim and a bit ethnic-looking, and I see on his nametag that he's Constable Coustas. They're both wearing those baseball-type police caps, which make them look a bit like teenagers.

'Psych ward, I think.'

'Really?' skinny woman says. She's a senior constable, but I miss her name. 'Where?'

'Dunno.'

Coustas glances at her, shrugs. 'We can check,' he says. 'Bit funny though, with the bank account and that.'

The senior constable opens her folder and takes my name and date of birth. She looks inside, over my shoulder.

'Live here?' she says.

'Not permanent. Not for much longer, I mean.'

'How do you know Miss Petrovic?'

'Who?'

'Miss Petrovic. Marietta Petrovic.'

Petrovic?

'I... I don't. I mean, not really. Steve invited us to stay for a bit. She was... already gone.'

Coustas takes over. 'Steve lives here, does he?'

'Yes... I—'

'Full name?'

'What?'

'Steve. What's his full name?'

'Ah... Petrovic. Steve Petrovic.'

Senior constable frowns. Looks at Coustas.

'Must be the brother,' she says. 'Parents said he might be about. Slava, I think it was.'

Brother?

Coustas frowns. 'Didn't think to tell the parents?'

'What?'

'About the psych ward.'

'I... I suppose not.'

'Where's he now?'

'Um, gone out. He'll be back later. What's this about?'

The senior constable takes off her cap. 'Mind if we come in?'

'What for?'

'Just a chat.'

'Aren't we already chatting?'

That probably sounds like I'm being a smartarse. But I don't think it's a good idea, in general, to invite cops inside. Especially if you don't know what they're looking for. Anton told me once that they need a warrant for that sort of thing, unless you invite them in. If it was Dirty Doug, that would be different, but I don't know either of these two.

Plus, there's the meth. Or whatever it is.

Coustas sniffs the air. 'What's that smell?'

Shit.

'What smell?'

She sniffs too, grimaces. 'Yeah. Like chlorine, or something. Or...'

'Dunno,' I say.

'C'mon,' Coustas says, 'we'll just come in for a minute.'

'Nah.'

The senior constable closes her folder, eyes harden. 'Listen, it's just a welfare check, right?'

'Welfare check?'

Coustas chimes in. 'Her parents live in the country. Bit worried because they haven't heard from her. Been trying to call, but phone's dead.'

'I um... I'll tell Steve then.'

They look at each other – quickly – facial expressions I can't quite place.

'Well, I'll give you a number he can call.' He hands me a card. 'Tell him to do it when he gets back, okay? Right away.'

'Likewise,' she says, 'if you've got any information—'

'Sure.'

I go to close the door, but the senior constable jams her foot in its way.

'Hang on a sec.'

I hold my breath.

Eyes search mine.

'What happened to your nose?'

'Gym. Aerobics class.'

Rolls her eyes. 'Right. Don't forget to call if—'

'I will. Definitely.'

I close the door, lean my back against it.

Slow, deep breaths in and out.

Her brother. Steve.

Slava.

* * *

The phone is attached to the wall, next to the fridge. One of those ugly-looking beige ones with grey numbers, like they have at Centrelink and places like that.

Anton reckons the old-style phones were nicer, with the dialler thing that you spun round. He said they just felt better in your hand, but you don't see those anywhere anymore, and they were before my time. With the old phones, he reckons, making a call seemed more important.

I pick up the handset. Completely dead – no dial tone, no sound. Nothing.

I follow the cord down the wall. It's nailed against the plaster with those little plastic brackets. And I see, down near the skirting board, the cord has been cut – frayed wires exposed.

An accident? Or maybe she just didn't want anyone to ring her? Could be loads of reasons, I suppose.

Loads of reasons.

My hands tremble.

Hot acid bile. Rises fast in my throat.

Slava.

Mary.

Maria.

Marietta.

The plastic drums.

thirty-two

Dirty Doug steps out into the foyer, stops halfway. Face drops.

'Jesus.'

'What?'

'Well, just look at you. You look like hell.'

I try to explain things, but my head is too mixed up – not making much sense.

He gets me a glass of water, tells me to slow down.

'I've been worried,' he says. 'Ages since I've seen you.'

The water is icy cold. I gulp it down too fast. It gives me brain-freeze.

'I need some help,' I say.

'No joke.'

'I've been trying to find Anton and—'

'What happened to your face?'

'Nothing. Doesn't matter.'

He sighs and sits down beside me. Stares straight ahead, crosses his arms.

'Still staying with Petrovic?'

I wonder whether to tell him about the welfare check, the phone, and whatever else. Maybe he already knows.

He takes a deep breath in and out.

'Keep away from him. Seriously.'

Finished the water. Want another.

He turns and faces me. 'Best to get out of there.'

'I know. I will.'

'How much you using?'

Don't tell him about the overdose. I shrug.

'And Petrovic?'

'What?'

'Using too?'

'Dunno.'

'Selling?'

'Don't think so.'

He unfolds his arms and leans back against the wall. I notice how shiny his shoes are. Black, almost like a mirror. I wonder if it's a rule or something, like in the army.

'Listen,' he says. 'I'm gonna tell you something.'

'But I really need to find out—'

'It's just hypothetical, right?'

'You'll help me find Anton?'

'Yep, but just listen for a minute.'

He leans forward and clasps his hands together. Linked fingers, facing straight ahead.

'Remember back a few years ago, when heroin was everywhere? When it was cheap?'

'Yeah.'

'And there was a heap of overdoses?'

I nod.

'Hypothetically, there might have been this bloke I investigated, who was dealing a fair bit back then.'

'Right.'

'But he was hard to nail, because he had this thing with cleaning the slate. Do you know what I mean by that?'

He turns and looks at me, eyes soften. Doesn't wait for an answer.

'Sometimes, when dealers get paranoid, they worry about their customers talking, you know?'

'Okay.'

'So when a bunch of users overdose, it sometimes looks a bit too convenient. You understand?'

The fluoro lights flicker.

'Think so.'

'Hard to prove, and there wasn't anyone making a stink about it. Families just figured they overdosed, and that was that.'

My stomach hurts, deep and low. Tightening, like a knot.

'He probably mixed something else in. Sedative, maybe. Combined with the smack, just too much. Hypothetically.'

I feel sick. Say nothing.

A young guy comes into the foyer, waits at the counter. A copper comes out quick.

'A few of his customers went missing altogether, so we could never be sure. Even took their bankcards, once or twice. Still, we thought it was mainly sadistic – not so much about money. But we never could prove anything about that. In the end, just easier to slot him for the dealing.'

The young guy has come to pick up a lost wallet. The copper tells him it's his lucky day. He smiles and agrees.

'I... do you know?'

'What?'

I turn to him. 'Is... is Anton okay?'

He sighs, stares at the floor.

'Yeah, he's okay. But he's in a lot of trouble.'

thirty-three

They call it MAP. The Melbourne Assessment Prison. Big red-brick place, down on Spencer Street.

Dirty Doug explained it's where you go before they decide where to send you longer term.

'No bed for him anywhere, so he'll be there a while. Remanded.'

He even rang the MAP people, which was pretty nice, just to let them know I was coming. Even so, it's fair to say the prison officers aren't especially friendly.

First, they make me go through some big machine that blows air on my skin. Apparently it can tell if I've got any drugs on me.

'If I had any,' I say, 'I wouldn't be bringing it here.'

A man with a very thick neck looks me up and down.

'Can't wear that,' he says.

'What?'

'That. You don't know what some of these blokes are like.' He goes behind a counter and brings me a t-shirt. 'Here.'

It's way too big, dark green, and has 'Bunnings' written on the front. It smells like detergent and is completely gross. They don't have a mirror, but I know I look ridiculous.

He smiles. 'All set then.'

I wait out in this big meeting room with lots of steel and plastic tables and chairs that are bolted down. There are two prison officers standing near the door, watching. Both chew gum. They look bored.

I study the people.

Try not to think about Steve. *Slava*. And what Dirty Doug told me.

At one table there's this skinny bloke, maybe in his twenties, and he's crying like a baby. A woman – who might be his mum – is rubbing his arm, which is pretty nice. She has deep, dark rings under her eyes. She smiles at me, grimly, yellow teeth of a smoker.

At the table next to me is an Islander girl with tatts on her chin. She's visiting some Islander guy who is probably the biggest person I've ever seen in my life. His arms thicker than my legs.

'What you getting for Mum?' he says.

He has a soft voice. Gentle. Not what I expected.

'What?' Big eyes. She's racing.

'Birthday's next week.'

'Is it?'

'Jeez, wake up, sis. You'll have to get something. From both of us, yeah?'

She nods, too many times, too fast. 'Flowers then, or what?'

I try to listen closely, to hear what they decide, and that's when Anton comes through the swinging doors. He pauses, the guards speak to him briefly, then he comes towards me.

God, it feels like ages. His skin looks a bit grey, but maybe it's the fluoro light.

'New job?'

He eyes my t-shirt.

'Like it?'

'Suits you.'

It feels good to see him smile, like this warm feeling rises up inside me. Fills me almost to the brim. So long since I felt that.

He sits opposite, and I put my hands out to his.

'How's it been?'

'Here?'

'Yeah.'

Shrugs. 'No dramas. You?'

'I'm okay.'

'You don't look so good.'

Should I tell him about Mary? What Dirty Doug said? I don't want him to worry, but—

'And Sunny?'

'What?'

'Sunny okay?'

I don't want to tell him that I let Steve take Sunny out. Somehow, it feels like a betrayal.

'He's home. At the flat, I mean. But we're gonna get out of there. Today.'

'Yeah?'

'Yeah. Just gotta go get him. Right after this.'

There's a small boy at one of the tables, with his mum. And he screams out like he's just so desperate to go home, more than anything in the world. I look at his dad, or brother, or whatever. He tries to smile, to calm him down. It doesn't work.

'Steve,' I say. 'He makes me nervous.'

Anton nods. 'You heard what happened?'

'Is it true?'

'Which bit?'

'Emilio?'

He shakes his head. 'I was there. But, you know.'

'Steve?'

Eyes cut away from me. 'Can't say.'

'Why?'

He leans forward, whispers. 'Can't say anything.'

'To me?'

'Anyone.'

'But it's me!'

He lets go of my hands. Crosses his arms. 'You don't get it. How it works in here.'

'Jesus, Anton.'

His hands are bruised, swollen. Angry-looking needle marks on his arms. They look fresh.

'Either way – him or me – doesn't matter. My word against his. And they'd still have me as an accessory.'

'Better though.'

Shakes his head. Coughs. 'I'd still be inside for a long time. And if I talk, it'll be hell. Might not make it out, you know? No good being a dog.'

He looks at me hard. I think about Steve and wonder whether that's always true.

'What are you gonna do then?'

'Plead guilty. With parole, might walk after fifteen. That's what the lawyer reckons.'

The Bunnings t-shirt is itching me almost everywhere, and I can tell he's already made up his mind. I know what he's like, with his rules.

It's what makes him who he is. It's pretty hard to break out of that, even if you know you really should. Even if it's probably ruining your life.

One of the prison officers shouts, *'Five minutes!'* much louder than he needs to, and it echoes around the room.

The little boy has stopped screaming, but he's still crying and pulling at his mum's jacket. She's trying to ignore him, to pretend everything is normal, but there's a terrible emptiness in her eyes. And you just know the brother – or husband, or whoever he is – can see it too.

Anton reaches over again, takes my hand.

'Definitely moving out, yeah?'

'What?'

'The flat.'

'Yep, just gonna get Sunny and I'm gone.'

'Good. The park?'

'Yep.'

'Be careful.'

'Of course.'

'Don't forget, you've still got to get that place for us, right?'

I try to smile.

'By the time I get out.'

'That'll be nice.'

'Do your zoo thing too.'

'Yep. For sure.'

'Promise?'

He squeezes my hand tight, reaches over and wipes the tears from my cheeks.

'Wrap it up!'

'I promise,' I say, and gently pull my hand from his. 'Definitely.'

thirty-four

I wouldn't have come back if it wasn't for Sunny. No way.
But I can't leave him, not with Steve.

The smell is what gets me this time, even worse than before
– still chemical, but there's something stronger underneath.

Thicker, sweeter.

Don't think about it.

I cover my nose, my mouth, and step inside. It's pretty
dark, so I turn on the light.

He's not back yet. Or Sunny.

Haven't worked out exactly what I'm going to say, but I'm
sure he won't care much. Probably happy to have the place
to himself again.

But I figure they can't be too much longer – it's almost
dark out, and I don't think he'll keep begging at night.

Sunny feels the cold, so I hope they won't be long.

* * *

Makes me edgy at the best of times – waiting around, I mean.
Like, no good usually comes of it.

But waiting for Steve, in the flat with the smell, is about a
hundred times worse. I try not to think about his room.

The drums.

Marietta.

All the usual crap is on TV. When I was a kid, I remember there used to be heaps of movies, even during the day. I used to like the old ones with Jerry Lewis and Dean Martin. Even the Elvis ones too – Mum used to let me watch them sometimes. He always seemed to be a racing car driver, or an astronaut, or something like that.

I don't remember much about my mum – brown curly hair, and these big soft eyes. I was only young when it happened.

One day, she went to the supermarket. I remember it was school holidays, so I was home on my own. She was gone for ages.

It wasn't until night-time that the police came. But they didn't tell me straight away. Instead, they took me to the station and there was this woman there who wasn't wearing a police uniform – she was the one who told me.

'There's been an accident,' she said.

And my mum wouldn't be coming home.

Sometimes, I wish I had a photo of her. I wish I had a photo so I could know exactly what she looked like. Especially her eyes, because that's what I try to remember most.

But sometimes, I'm not sure if I do remember. Your mind can play tricks on you like that – she might have looked completely different.

And sometimes, I wonder if maybe it was like Anton's mum. Sometimes, I wonder if maybe it wasn't an accident at all.

* * *

It's completely dark now outside.

I found a movie on one of the channels. The foreign channel, SBS. It's one I've seen before with Anton – we saw it at the convent. The one the German hippies told us to go see.

Pan's Labyrinth.

Like I said, we both thought it was an excellent movie,

and the only thing we disagreed about was what happened at the end.

I'll try not to spoil it (in case you haven't seen it), but I thought the little girl *did* go live with her mother and father, and everything worked out because she'd done exactly as the magical faun had told her. So she became Princess Moanna.

But Anton reckoned the magical faun and that whole thing was 'just her imagination', because she couldn't deal with what was happening in real life.

I could see how that might make sense, but I thought it was a pretty pessimistic way of looking at it. Anton said he was 'just being realistic'.

Either way, we still both agreed it was a pretty great movie – especially because you could see the ending in different ways.

Anyway, it's about halfway through now, and I decide I'll try to watch the rest of it from Anton's point of view. Like, that the little girl – whose name is Ofelia – that she's imagining the faun, the puzzles, and all of that part of it – that none of it is actually real.

To be honest, it's kind of beautiful to watch it like that. So I can understand what Anton meant. In some ways, it's much more beautiful. But it's also much more sad.

Then I see it on the coffee table.

It's only a small bag.

Not much inside.

Maybe just enough.

I pick it up and hold it to the light – definitely enough for one hit.

Steve must have left it by mistake. Or maybe he came back after scoring, and this was my share. That's most likely. It's not the sort of thing you'd leave around by accident.

But it makes me wonder where he's gone with Sunny. Maybe he's gone to buy more gear. Maybe this was all he could get.

I hope Sunny is okay.

It's pretty distracting, sitting there like that. Like, I could do with a touch, just to settle my nerves.

Might help me be calmer about talking to Steve. About telling him I'm leaving. Might make things a bit easier.

Everything else fades to the background, like a black-and-white movie, but we're left in colour – just me and the gear.

We're all that's left.

The movie is nearly over, so I decide I should wait to the end. If I wait to the end, then I can have it. A reward. Plus, Steve and Sunny might be back by then, so I can be sure it was meant for me.

So I watch and I wait till the end.

* * *

Somehow, maybe for the first time ever, it feels good to cry.

And it's better to be outside, with the cool air going deep into my lungs. Outside and away from what's there. Away from everything.

I can feel it now.

I know it.

Sunny isn't coming back.

And so I run.

I run as fast as I can.

Soon, I'm far away from the flat.

From Steve.

And everything.

My breaths are raw and wild, and the tears eventually stop.

I'm heading somewhere. I don't know where, not exactly, but it feels right. People look at me funny, but I don't care anymore, because I'm going somewhere better.

Eventually, when I'm out of breath, I stop.

Look around.

Lygon Street, up near the cemetery.

A tram rattles past. All the cars and the lights and the people – like a river that never stops.

I look for the house. The one where the graffiti was.

The one Anton said he painted, but I never believed him.

And it's as beautiful as I remember.

But someone has made it even better.

I never realised it was only part of the story, that it wasn't quite finished.

Maybe Anton didn't know the rest.

Didn't know the ending.

And even though it's in a different colour, and the writing is different, it's so much better now.

It's better because it's finished, and it makes more sense.

It's like in the movies – how everything can be fixed in the end.

It's never too late.

I'll have to tell Anton what it says.

And I'll show him too, when he gets out.

He'll love it, because it was beautiful before.

But now, it's perfect—

THE WORLD IS SICK

SO KISS ME QUICK

* * *

Chest aches. Lungs are burning.

I wipe tears from my cheeks and reach inside my pocket.

It's there.

Must've known I might need it.

Anton said once that your subconscious knows things better than your conscious mind.

'Sometimes,' he said, 'it knows what's good for you, even if you don't.'

I've never really understood what he meant by that, and I'm not sure he did either.

'Your subconscious calls the shots,' he said, 'even when you think you're in charge.'

So maybe that's why.

Maybe my subconscious made me bring it.
Maybe, this time, Anton was right.
I take it out.
Crumpled and bent.
Unfold it carefully, straighten the edges.
A deep breath.
In and out.
And I go looking for a phone box.

after

thirty-five

I wake before the sun.

I'd set my alarm and everything, but there was really no need.

The train leaves at seven, so I still have plenty of time.

I put the light on in the kitchen, make my breakfast. I've got one of those stovetop coffee makers now, like Italians use. I got it from the Brotherhood for five bucks, and it was almost brand new.

The coffee is strong, but delicious.

I sit and listen to the wind through the gum tree out back – there's just one out there, an enormous thing that creaks and sways. The neighbour told me it will come down one day, surely.

'Be the end of you,' he said.

He said it on the day I moved in, and hasn't uttered a word since. That's fine by me, though. I like the quiet and I like the house. It's small, but the garden is wild, and I sit out there sometimes and listen to the birds. I feel the cold air on my skin and breathe it deeply into my lungs.

It reminds me.

I finish my coffee as the morning birds start up, letting each other know who's still around after a long, cold night. Most nights are cold up here, which I don't mind so much. There's a fireplace and the wood is cheap.

I get dressed slowly, layer upon layer. I've learned it's the best way to keep warm. Mornings are the hardest though. Living in a house has made me a bit soft like that.

It wasn't really my choice – to come to Ballarat, I mean. If I had a say, it'd be somewhere like Byron Bay, even if I've never been there before. Or maybe Hervey Bay, like that woman talked about once.

I'd only ever been to Ballarat once before, and that was in primary school. We'd come to Sovereign Hill, which was all about the gold rush and that kind of thing. It was pretty good, from what I can remember. We even got dressed up in the old-timey clothes, which was kind of ridiculous.

But they got a house for me – a proper house. I think Dirty Doug must have pulled some strings after the court case, because the Centrelink people were nice for once, and it all got sorted pretty quick. It didn't matter about the last time, which I'd been worried about. They lined me up for some rehab too.

Dirty Doug said it would be good for me, to move I mean. Especially after Steve and everything. He reckoned the country air would do me wonders. Plus, the court case had been in the papers and on the news a lot. Seemed like everyone knew about it. What Steve had done.

'Best to get out of the city,' Dirty Doug said, 'after everything that's happened.'

And he was probably right about that.

* * *

The train station is a big old thing, really grand-looking. A lot of Ballarat is like that, from the olden days and the gold rush. Really ornate and beautiful buildings. Big hotels and that sort of stuff. Nice wide streets too.

Looks like there's only one other person catching the train, an old lady with one of those vinyl shopping carts with wheels. She's nicely dressed with a green woollen coat and matching hat. She has a sparkly-looking brooch on her lapel, which looks like a peacock.

'Hello,' she says.

Breath steams.

'Hi.'

'Off to Melbourne then?'

That's pretty obvious, seeing as we're both waiting on the platform for the same train. But it's no good being a smartarse about it. I've learned how country people like to 'make conversation', as they say.

'Visiting someone.'

She smiles, and I can tell she's waiting for me to ask.

'You?'

'Oh, just passing time. The Victoria Market for a few things, that's all.'

I reckon it's a long trip just to go to the market, but don't say so.

'That's nice.'

She nods. She glances back at me, her eyes strain and she squints.

'You look familiar.'

'Yeah?'

I wonder if she recognises me from the news. The court case.

'You work in one of the shops?'

I'm relieved it isn't about Steve, which has happened a few times. Less and less now, though. People forget.

'Coles. Just part-time.'

. She claps her hands once. 'Knew it! I never forget a face!'

Thing is, working a checkout, you see a lot of people, and you don't remember hardly any of them. They remember you, though. And sometimes, even remember your name. Mainly because of the nametag.

'It's Danielle, isn't it?'

I nod. 'Yep, but people call me Dani.'

I can hear the train approaching from the distance, a low

and heavy hum, and I hope she doesn't end up sitting next to me. She seems nice enough, but I don't really feel like talking that much. Maybe it's living alone that's done it. I've gotten used to the quiet.

In general, I'd say Ballarat people are different than in Melbourne, but not super-friendly either. In the street they look at you and nod. Some might smile, or even say hello. That's different than in the city, for sure.

I think people in the city are a bit scared of each other. Not like they're worried they'll get stabbed or anything, but maybe scared of connecting. It's like people already have their friends and their families, and they don't want or need anyone else.

Ballarat people are different though, because I think they understand that sometimes it's nice to say hello. It feels good to acknowledge another person, and to be acknowledged, if you know what I mean.

But, like I said, it still isn't super-friendly or anything. It isn't like one of those British TV shows where people move to a little village, and everyone is jolly and they all get in romances and adventures. Those shows are so ridiculous. Honestly, most of what's on TV is just terrible.

* * *

The sky has darkened by the time I get there – the weather closed in. Luckily, from Fawkner Station, it isn't far to walk.

The houses are packed in tight together, neat homes with empty driveways. Their neighbours, over the road, are the quietest in Melbourne. I wonder if it's depressing – seeing all that death. Or if maybe it makes them appreciate things more – like it's a reminder that we're not here forever.

The place is enormous – so much bigger than Carlton. It's all different, newer, with a grand-looking gate and manicured lawns.

I walk through row upon row of old Italians and Greeks

– Mazzucco, Nicolini, Kokkinou – with marble like they probably would never have known in their lifetimes. Maybe it's human nature – we always try to make up for things. Our failings. Mostly when it's too late.

The office. A pale woman – almost sickly. Gentle eyes and a smile that almost makes up for the place.

'Who you looking for, love?'

It's the thing I've probably noticed most, since being clean. People are nicer, and don't assume the worst. You could definitely get away with a lot more, but probably don't need to.

She taps away at a keyboard, her face lit blue-grey by the monitor. She doesn't ask if I'm a relative, or a friend, or anything. I'd been ready for that, but I suppose it doesn't matter when you're dead, does it? I mean, anyone can visit you. Even your enemies.

She swivels the monitor around to face me – a map. Points to the far left corner, near the road. Traces her finger to the spot.

'Row 14, Section DD,' she says. 'Driving?'

'No.'

She looks out the window. 'Better be quick then. Bit dire out there.'

I thank her, turn for the door.

'Wait,' she stands up. 'Shift finishes soon enough. How about I drive you?'

* * *

Rain comes hard and heavy, thudding dully against the windscreen. The wipers swish silently, left and right.

'What's it like?' I say.

'What's what like?'

'Working here?'

She smiles. 'Get asked that a lot.'

'And?'

'I like it. I mean, of course it's sad to see people upset.

It can be terrible, especially with young ones. But, I get to help people, you know? Make it a bit easier. More bearable, I suppose. Even just in a small way.'

The road is thin and smooth, and it snakes delicately through the rows of headstones. It's unimaginable how many are buried here. She drives slowly, almost respectfully, even if it seems like there's no one else around. We pass enormous crypts, the size of houses, with colours of marble I've never seen.

'Impressive, aren't they?' she says.

'Have you ever—'

'Inside?' She nods. 'Get asked that a lot too. Most are like little chapels, you know? Statues of Mary, Jesus, angels – all that. I guess people want to do everything they can. Makes them feel better.'

The rain begins to ease and she turns the car onto a still narrower road, leading to a part of the cemetery where graves are sparse, trees smaller, and the rumble of Sydney Road is within earshot.

'Fairly new here,' she says. 'Keep expanding, of course.'

She pulls the car over to a grassy embankment. Cuts the engine.

'This it?' I say.

Nods. 'You want me to come?'

'No, it's fine. I won't be long.'

Her eyes soften. 'Take your time.'

* * *

The wind is stronger now, colder, and the rain has stopped. The sun has broken through, but gives little warmth.

There's no headstone, just a plain wooden cross. The numbers 35464 stamped in its middle. No name. The soil still seems fresh and dark. A few thin weeds poke through meekly.

I close my eyes.

First, his smile.

Then, him tickling me on a crisp winter's morning.

Sunny's warmth between us.

And, if I listen hard enough, the sounds of the morning birds in Princes Park.

All of it, it comes to me.

He once said that life was a 'zero-sum game'. He'd heard about it on the radio – it's where one person's success means someone else has to fail. Or something like that. And it kind of makes sense, in a way.

Still, I don't want to believe it – it seems too harsh, too cruel.

Anton didn't die because life is a 'zero-sum game' – he didn't die so someone else could live. He just got caught in a rip – too strong, too deep – he couldn't hold on any longer.

I wish I'd brought something, some flowers maybe, even if he was never into that type of thing. Something just to show I'd been here. So if anyone else comes, they won't think they're the first. They won't think he's been forgotten.

I'll come back, though. And when I do, I'll bring flowers. Maybe a picture of the house. I know he'll be happy for me – he'll be happy it happened, that I made it.

I feel better just to think of it.

And maybe, down the track, I'll get him a proper headstone too. If I save some money, I can at least get something with his name on it, and some kind of inscription – a message.

I know exactly what it should say.

So people will know.

* * *

Back inside the car, the lady turns to me.

She puts her hand on mine and squeezes, her skin soft and warm. It feels good.

'You were close?'

I nod. Wipe my cheeks.

She sighs. 'Hard to say goodbye, isn't it?'

She hands me a tissue, starts the car.

'Where you headed?'

I clear my throat. 'Ballarat.'

She smiles. 'Just a bit out of my way. Train station?'

'I don't want to be a trouble.'

'No trouble.'

The car goes through the gates and pulls out slowly onto Sydney Road. I power the window down and let the wind rush in. The air is cool, but fresh and new from the rain-slicked streets. I breathe in deeply. Feel it in my chest.

I close my eyes and tell myself that everything has changed.

I'll never go back to how things were.

For Anton.

For Marietta.

For Sunny.

For me.

And I will make myself believe it.

acknowledgements

Deepest thanks to my publisher, Vanessa Radnidge, and to Grace Heifetz at Curtis Brown. Thanks also to Deonie Fiford, Stacey Clair and Boyd Spradbury for your insights.

Thank you to Louise Sherwin-Stark, Fiona Hazard, Justin Ractliffe, Dan Pilkington, Klara Zak, Thomas Saras, Andrew Cattanach, and the exceptional team at Hachette Australia – your support means so much.

Finally, I am grateful to family and friends (who forgive my absences), and to Millie, Bridie (and Sunny) – forever at my side.